A King Production presents…

Baller Bitches
VOLUME 1

A NOVEL

JOY DEJA KING

ISBN 13: 978-0986004520

ISBN 10: 0986004529

Cover concept by Deja King & www.MarionDesigns.com
Cover layout and graphic design by www.MarionDesigns.com
Typesetting: Keith Saunders
Editors: Suzy McGlown and Linda Williams

Library of Congress Cataloging-in-Publication Data;
A King Production
Baller Bitches Volume 1: a series/by Joy Deja King
For complete Library of Congress Copyright info visit;
www.dejaking.com

A KING PRODUCTION

A King Production
P.O. Box 912, Collierville, TN 38027

A King Production and the above portrayal log are trademarks of
A King Production LLC

Dedication

This Book is Dedicated To My:
Family, Readers and Supporters.
I LOVE you guys so much. Please believe that!!

Baller Bitches

VOLUME 1

A NOVEL

JOY DEJA KING

Diamond

"Bitch, you ain't shit!" When my baby daddy stood in front of me screaming that bullshit with spit flying everywhere, I kept putting the clear coat of polish on my nails ignoring his ass. "Did you hear what the fuck I said?" he belted as the vein in the middle of his forehead started pulsating.

"Mutherfucka, everybody in the damn building can hear what the fuck you just said. Are you done ranting 'cause I got shit to do?"

"That's what's wrong wit yo' ass, yo' mouth too fuckin' slick."

"Umm this shit gettin' repetitive. Ain't but so many ways you can call me a bitch and tell me I ain't shit. I get it, you think I'm foul. So either come up with some new descriptions or move on to something else."

"I can't believe I got a baby wit' yo' stupid ass. You don't give a fuck about nobody but yourself. One day I promise I'ma take our daughter away from you because I refuse to let her grow up and end up like you."

I put my polish down and eyeballed Rico because I wanted him to know what I was about to say wasn't a game. "Nigga, the day you start plotting to take my daughter away from me is the day you better tell yo' mama to start making your funeral arrangements. You can call me every ho, dick sucker, no good bitch all mutherfuckin' day but when you bring Destiny into the mix we have a problem. Now please get the fuck out my crib and take that noise you spewing someplace else."

"Diamond, this shit ain't over. I'll be back tomorrow to pick up my daughter for the weekend and she better be here and not at your mother's house."

"I tell you what. Why don't you pick Destiny up from my mother's house tomorrow because I can't take having to see yo' ass two days in a row."

"No, I'll pick Destiny up from here tomorrow. So whatever partying and fucking you planning on doing tonight make sure you have yo' ass up in time to get my daughter in the morning."

"That's what your problem is now. So busy worrying about what the fuck I'm doing," I huffed under my breath not wanting to reignite the argument because I was ready for Rico to bounce. "Bye," I said keeping my head down, until I heard the door shut.

There was a time an argument with Rico would fuck up my entire day but this shit had become so routine I barely broke a sweat over it now. See, there was a time when Rico was actually my boyfriend. I thought we would be together forever but that was when I was young and dumb. He swooped me up when I was fifteen and not used to good dick or money. When I was walking home from school one afternoon he pulled up in a tricked out Benz and I couldn't believe when he rolled down the window asking me for my name. He was one of those pretty niggas who knew his packaging was right.

From that day on we started dating. Rico would pick me up from school almost everyday and them chick's mouths dropped every time he pulled up and I would get in the car. We would go get something to eat and just talked. Although he was three years older than me he never made me feel like a kid instead I felt like a woman. But I wasn't a woman and Rico was way out of my league. He quickly made me his girl but that didn't keep him from having mad other bitches, so many I couldn't keep count. In the beginning I fell for all his lies. He had a valid excuse for every accusation I had. By the time I woke up to the truth it was two years later and I was pregnant with Destiny.

That was the roughest nine months of my life. I had bitches calling my phone harassing me. They would say my man just left their crib and he fucked the shit out of them. My feet swelled up, belly poked out feeling depressed and helpless having to hear this shit. By this time, Rico wasn't even trying to hide his dirt anymore. He felt I was pregnant and stuck. Even after all that I stayed with Rico. It took another year before I wised up and gave that nigga the deuces. When I did Rico tried to make my life a living hell. I guess he thought I would be a dumbass forever...not!

I spent the first year of Destiny's life being with her day and night while Rico ran the streets. I don't even remember him changing one diaper. But I loved her so much it didn't even matter. Destiny was like my real life baby doll and she helped me get my shit together. I had gained so much weight during my pregnancy and even more afterwards and I think it was out of depression, because Rico had me so stressed out. I decided I had to get myself back on point and I started taking Destiny out in her stroller everyday. Within six months I had walked all that weight off. After that you couldn't tell me nothing, including Rico. I went from being a sad, miserable bitch to a baller bitch.

Kennedy

"Kennedy, I need you to read over this carefully," my boss, Darcy said, handing me two pieces of paper. As I sat in my cubicle, I looked over the agenda. I was an account executive at a PR/Event Planning firm and there was a long laundry list of things I was supposed to handle for the charity event tonight. I had so much to do I barely had time to go home and change clothes but due to past experiences I learned to always keep a few outfits with me. Darcy was notorious for waiting to the very last minute to give me a shitload of things to do and have me scrambling to get it all done.

So here I was, shaking my head wondering how I would pull this off and still look halfway decent doing it. But somehow, someway I would—I always did and it probably was due to the fact this had always been my dream job. When I was in college, I interned at just about every PR firm in New York hoping one would lead to a full time position. But working for Darcy Woods was always my #1 choice.

She was the rep for all the young, hip stars, which turned her into a celebrity herself. If you saw a star on the red carpet most of the time you would see Darcy standing right next to them looking like a star too. So when she offered me the position as an account executive, I jumped at it although it paid the least out of all my other job offers. But it was worth taking a low salary if it meant working under the queen herself or so I initially thought. But I quickly found out that the reason Darcy was able to be so cool, in control and look on point was because she delegated the work to everybody else and it freed up her time to mingle and be fabulous. But I also figured that was why her turnover rate was so high, because her employees would get burnt out and quit. With the money she was paying there wasn't much motivation to stay. None of that mattered to me though because I was determined to learn all I could from Darcy before going anywhere and I felt I was well on my way.

"Tammy, I need you to go down this list and confirm that the press covering this event have their proper credentials and know what time they should arrive at the venue."

"No problem, is there anything else you need me to do?"

"That's it for now but let me know when you're finished as there is definitely more to follow."

"Whatever you need, I got you," she smiled. Tammy was my saving grace. She was my intern and she busted her ass like she was making a big boy salary. When I was stuck in the office working to ten or eleven o'clock at night, Tammy was right there with me. I called her my co-pilot.

As I started getting my stuff together so I could head over to the venue to make sure the seating for the celebrities was correct I heard my cell ringing. "Hey, Diamond, what's going on?"

"Girl, you sound stressed."

"You know how it is on event day...hectic. So what time are you coming tonight?"

"That's why I was calling you to see what time I should come?"

"I think eight is good."

"Cool and can I bring my cousin?"

"Diamond, I already told you I can only get you in and I'm sneaking doing that shit. You know how Darcy is."

"I know but you know I had to ask again. You know I hate going to this shit alone and you're always way to busy to kick it with me."

"Girl, you always end up seeing somebody you know or some guy be up under you all night so you'll be fine. I would love to chat but work calls."

"No problem, see you tonight."

When I got off the phone with Diamond, I motioned for Tammy to come on. She could make her calls while on the move. This business taught you to do multiple things. While Tammy was handling press calls I was speaking to artist's managers on one phone and responding to text messages about the event on the other. This event was a major deal for Darcy and everything had to go smoothly. She was used to doing events for rappers and singers, but this was the first time she had scored an A list actress. Mega superstar Tyler Blake was hosting a star-studded charity event for Autism Awareness Month. Darcy bragged for two weeks straight when the gig was sealed and I was right there cheering her on. See, after grinding my ass off for over a year my hard work had finally paid off. I played an intricate part in securing the deal for Darcy and she promised me a commission for doing so. All I had to do was make sure the event went smoothly and I was micromanaging every detail to make sure that happened.

"Can you take us to the Soho House on Ninth Avenue," I directed the driver when we got in the cab.

"All the press has been confirmed. None of them seem to have any intentions on missing this event."

"Yeah, this is definitely the biggest gig Darcy has ever had. I haven't had so many calls from managers and agents trying to get their clients on the guest list. I had to explain to them that the tables have all been sold out for weeks. It's literally standing room only and that's full to capacity. Unless it's President Obama, I can't get anybody else in."

"Darcy, will be pleased to know that."

"You know it! She lives to be able to tell people they can't get in," I laughed.

"So what do you need for me to do when we get to the venue?"

"The first thing is making sure the table placement is correct. I made sure to sit certain celebs next to each other and keep others away. We don't need any drama."

"I got you."

After paying the cab we headed inside to the 4th floor where the private ballroom booked for the event was located. When we stepped off the elevator the craziness was in full effect. There were workers everywhere putting the final touches on the décor and making sure security was extra tight.

"Let's go check on the tables."

"Kennedy, the layout is gorgeous," Tammy commented as we walked into the room. "You totally made the right choice with the peach and cream colors. It's beautiful."

"It did turn out even better than I thought it would."

"Is Darcy here, I know she must love it."

"No, she sent me a text. She's doing the red carpet so she won't be here until the event is about to start."

"Luckily she has you to oversee everything. You basically put this entire event together yourself."

"Thanks, but luckily I have you. You've helped me out tremendously. So let's get to it because I

have a feeling this will be a night we'll never forget."
I didn't give a damn what I had to do I wanted to
make sure this event went off without a glitch. Yes,
this was Darcy's company and she was the boss, but
one day I knew I would be a boss too and everything
I did was preparing me for that.

Blair

"Is that what you're planning on wearing tonight?" When Michael asked me the question I just stood there for a second and didn't say anything.

"Yes, why you don't like it?"

"Out of all the clothes I've bought you, that's the best you could come up with? You need to go find something a little more sophisticated to put on." I looked down at the short lavender dress I had on. I spent all day yesterday looking for something to wear and when I found this dress I thought it would be perfect for the event tonight but clearly Michael didn't agree.

"I'll go change. Give me a minute."

"Hurry up, I don't want to be late." As I walked to my bedroom all the excitement I had been feeling only a few minutes earlier disappeared.

When Michael first told me I would be attending the charity event with him I felt like I must've been dreaming. He was a well sought after entertainment attorney, so we attended a ton of really nice industry events but this one tonight was super exclusive and for the last two weeks all I had been thinking about was what I would wear to something so special. But as always Michael had found a way to ruin my joy.

I practically ripped off the lavender dress I was wearing and threw it on the floor. I then picked it up and tossed it in the trashcan. I wanted it out of my face. It was nothing but a bad reminder of the shortcomings Michael thought I had. I walked over to my closet and pulled out one of the black cocktail dresses Michael had gotten for me. I slipped it on and did a quick glance in the mirror before going back out.

"Now that's more like it," Michael smiled.

"Maybe you should just start picking out my clothes for me every time we go out."

"Do I detect an attitude?'

"I just don't understand what was wrong with the other dress I had on."

"After all these months of us being together, I would think you would've learned the difference between trash and class but obviously I'm wrong."

"That dress wasn't trashy."

"Blair, you're a pseudo model. You know nothing about real class. I'm trying to teach you but that attitude of yours is making it difficult. Now lets go. We're already running late."

As we sat in the back of the chauffer driven car I had to fight back the tears that wanted to flow out my eyes. A part of me wanted to give into my pain but I refused to but it was becoming more and more difficult. Maybe part of the pain came from the fact that I felt Michael was right about me. When we met I was barely getting by. I was waiting tables, trying to become an actress. Let's just say the roles weren't rolling in so I took up some bullshit modeling gigs that practically paid no money, hoping it would give me some exposure and in a way it did because I did meet Michael. That would've never happened under normal circumstances because we definitely didn't run in the same circles. But one day I was doing a photo shoot with a rapper that Michael was the attorney for. He had to stop by and get him to sign some papers. I guess the two-piece bikini I was wearing caught his eye because he left there with the signed papers and my phone number.

I was stunned he was even interested in me. He had the looks of a young Denzel Washington and the brains of Obama but after some time, I would learn he could also be cruel like a cold-blooded killer. The first time we went out he took me to this elegant restaurant that had things on the menu I couldn't even pronounce. It amazed me how he could talk about Fortune 500 companies but relate to the streets. He was everything I grew up believing I would never find in a man and if I did he wouldn't want me because I wasn't good enough.

My grandmother on my father's side raised me in Harlem. My mother was young and didn't want to be bothered with me so when I was six she dropped me off with my father and never came back. He was a hustler and made a lot of money. He took good care of his mother, so she had no problem taking care of me. But when I was eleven he got robbed and killed. My grandmother was devastated. I wasn't sure if it was because her son was dead or her money supply ran out because after he was gone it was like she didn't want to be bothered with me. I basically ended up raising myself. So having a man like Michael show interest gave me a feeling of worth but it came at a high price.

"We're here. Let's go." As we stepped out the car there were photographers everywhere and they were all going crazy taking pictures of Tyler Blake. She was one of the highest paid actresses in Hollywood and hands down the biggest black actress. I remember the first movie I saw her in. She was my inspiration to try and break into the business. Watching Tyler Blake work the red carpet she made it seem so easy, but I knew making it in that business was much harder than anybody could anticipate.

By the time we finally made it inside to the event I had seen just about every A list celebrity from the movie, music and sports world and of course Michael knew them all. As always I played my position and stepped to the side while he mingled. As one of the waitresses was walking by I took a glass of champagne off the tray. Being around so much glitz and glamour had me feeling completely inadequate. I was hoping a few glasses of bubbly would take the edge off.

"OMG, Blair, what are you doing here?"

"Diamond, hey!" I said giving her a hug. "You look great! I love your dress."

"You look good too! A little conservative for my taste but still good," she smiled. I couldn't help but laugh because I felt the same way. "So what are you doing here?"

"I came with Michael."

"So you still with that attorney dude?" I nodded my head yes. "Damn, that's why I can't get you on the phone no more."

"I know it's been awhile. I miss you."

"I miss you too but girl, that's a good look. That man fine and rich."

"Yeah, so how 'bout you. Who did you come with," I asked not wanting to discuss Michael any further.

"My home girl is working the event. I don't think you've ever met Kennedy. She's a workaholic. She's about her business. She managed to get me an invite but she could only get me one so I had to come solo."

"I would love if you could sit with us because besides you and Michael I don't know anybody here and as you can see he's nowhere to be found."

"I'll see if Kennedy can work something out. Maybe she can do some switching of the seats. Oh shit, there she is...Kennedy," Diamond called out getting her attention."

"Diamond, when did you get here?"

"A few minutes ago. This is my friend, Blair."

"How did you get her in here? I told you, you couldn't bring anybody."

"Girl, calm yo' ass down. Blair came with somebody else, she didn't come with me."

"Oh, I know you always trying something."

"I know tonight's important, so I didn't try nothing but I was hoping you could help us out."

"With what?"

"Can you get us to sit next to each other at the same table?"

"Where are you sitting at?"

"I'm not sure, my boyfriend has the invitations."

"What's his name?"

"Michael Frost."

"The attorney...wow! He represents all the heavy hitters."

"I told her that was a good look," Diamond chimed in.

"I know what table you're at. That won't be a problem. I can maneuver something."

"You're the best! I knew you would work it out for us."

"Whatever, let me go work some magic. I'll be right back."

"I'm glad she was able to come through. I was

dreading keeping myself company while Michael talked to everybody but me."

"No worries, I'm here now and check out the cuties coming our way," Diamond smiled, nudging my arm.

"How are you ladies doing?"

"We're good."

"I'm Cameron and this is Kirk."

"I'm Diamond and this is Blair."

"So are you ladies here alone?"

"I am," Diamond said quickly.

"I'm here with my boyfriend."

"That's too bad," the dude Kirk said in a low tone.

"That doesn't mean we can't all still be friends," Cameron stated.

"Exactly. Ain't nothing wrong with a little friendship," Diamond agreed. "Does that mean you want my number?"

"Only if I can give you mine too." I laughed to myself as Diamond and Cameron exchanged numbers. Diamond had changed so much in the last few years, but I admired how she was doing her and didn't give a fuck what nobody thought.

"So you don't think that maybe we can exchange numbers too?"

"I don't think my boyfriend would like that."

"I don't see a ring on your finger so it can't be that serious."

"It's serious enough."

"Well, if you change your mind…"

"Kirk, Cameron, it's good to see you." Michael said walking up on us cutting Kirk off mid sentence.

"Hey Mike, it's good to see you my man," both of them said shaking Michael's hand. They engaged in some small talk for a few minutes before he turned to me.

"Let's go to our table and sit down," Michael said taking my hand. As we were about to walk away, I caught the shocked look on Kirk's face and realized it wasn't until that moment he knew I was with him.

"I'll be over there in a few," Diamond told me as she wrapped things up with Cameron.

"How do you know Cameron and Kirk?" Michael asked me as we made our way to the table.

"I don't. They came over and introduced themselves to me and Diamond."

"I see." When Michael gave short responses like that it meant he didn't approve. But then again Michael didn't approve of much of anything that he didn't tell me to do.

I was so happy when Diamond came and sat down next to me because Michael basically ignored me for the rest of the night. Everything was a one or two word response. Luckily the champagne kept flowing and I entertained myself by sizing up all the celebrities in attendance. At that moment I decided it was time for a major change in my life. Instead of stargazing, somehow I would become a star myself and get the respect I yearned for from Michael.

Diamond

All morning I was in a bad fuckin' mood. I had to get up mad early and pick Destiny up from my mother's crib because Rico was coming over to get her. He could've picked her up from my mother's place himself but of course that would mean making my life a lot easier and he tried to avoid that at all cost. After Destiny and I got back home I even tried to lie down for a little while to get some more sleep, but Rico started blasting my phone letting me know he was on the way. For a second I regretted even going to that event last night until I looked down at my phone and saw the text message from Cameron. A smile instantly crossed my face and the headache I had was starting to fade. When I was about to text Cameron back I saw that Blair was calling.

"Hey girl, what's going on?"

"Not too much. It was so good seeing you last night."

"I know. We both be so busy we don't ever

have time to hang out anymore. We used to see each other at least once a week. But I understand. You gotta man now and shit done change. It's cool."

"No it's not. Trust me, no man can replace the fun you have with your girlfriends. That's why I was hoping we could have lunch or dinner today to catch up."

"I would love to."

"Great, and you can bring Destiny. I haven't seen her in what seems like forever."

"I would but I'm actually waiting for her dad now to pick her up."

"How is Rico doing?"

"The same but we can wait to discuss him when we play catch up at lunch." Both of us laughed, as Blair was well aware of our drama.

"Can't wait. So what time do you want to meet and where?"

"Probably in a couple of hours. I'll send you a text after Rico gets Destiny and confirm everything."

"Cool, see you soon." When I hung up with Blair I anxiously texted Cameron back and ended it with a smiley face. For a quick second an image of Cameron and I walking holding hands, being in love flashed through my mind. I couldn't help but fall back on my bed and laugh. After all the bullshit I'd been through with Rico and the rest of the slick ass niggas I dated after him, I was still a romantic at heart. As I continued laughing the knocking at the door brought that shit to a halt. I rolled my eyes dreading to see Rico.

"Come on, Destiny, your daddy is here," I said in a fake cheerful voice. As much as I couldn't stand her daddy I didn't want Destiny to know it. So I pretended to be happy when he came to pick her up but he was beginning to make the task more and more difficult because he was no longer going along with the program. He would say foul shit to me under his breath purposely trying to fuck with me. Destiny couldn't really understand what he meant but the tension was getting obvious. So now I would have Destiny in hand at the door so there wouldn't even be a need for him to step foot in my crib. It was like cash and carry, get your daughter and carry her out.

"Hi Daddy," Destiny smiled when I opened the door. I quickly handed her to him.

"Hey, pretty girl," he said using Destiny to invite himself in. With Destiny in hand he brushed passed me and signaled for his homeboy to come in too.

"What's all this? I got things to do. You all need to go 'head and leave," I frowned eyeballing Rico and his friend with the small tat on his neck.

"Is that anyway to talk to the father of your child. Isn't that right, Destiny," he said kissing her on the cheek.

This nigga here stay fuckin' wit' me. If only my

dumbass hadn't got caught up in some good dick and curly hair, I thought to myself. "Listen, Rico, I really do have things to do."

"Things like what?"

"Cleaning up...things like that," I lied. It was none of his fucking business but I wasn't going to say that in front of Destiny.

"You don't even know how to clean up," he chuckled with his friend joining in. It was bad enough I had to tolerate Rico but dealing with his friend was about to send me over the edge. I didn't like motherfuckers I didn't know in my crib and now the dude wanted to laugh, it was all too much.

"Rico, it's time for you to go. I love you, Destiny," I said walking over and giving her a kiss. "I'll see you later on tonight."

"My mom's wants to take Destiny to Jasmine's birthday party tomorrow so I'll bring her back home after that."

"Cousin Jazzy party, fun!" Destiny smiled with her eyes widening in excitement. Destiny loved her some Jasmine.

"That's fine. Just call me when you're on your way back." With swiftness I was at the door holding it open. I was trying to stop any chance of a continuing conversation. Rico stood looking at me for a few seconds before taking his time to walk out. His friend seemed to take even longer.

"Bye, Mommy," Destiny waved and I waved

back while smiling. When they were out I closed the door behind me and leaned against it for a sec until I heard my cell ring. When I reached it I saw it was Cameron calling.

"Hello."

"Hey, you were taking so long to respond to my text, you left me no choice but to call you."

"Sorry about that. I was taking care of something and didn't realize you had hit me back."

"That's okay. It worked out for the best. I get to hear your voice." I giggled, feeling like I was in junior high or some shit. "So what you getting into today?"

"I'm actually about to meet my friend Blair for lunch."

"The girl you were with last night?"

"Yes."

"We should all go out to dinner tonight. I know Kirk would like to see her again and I definitely want to see you."

"I would like that."

"Good. So I'll call you later on and let you know what time I'll pick you up."

"Works for me, bye." Man I was cheesing so hard, I felt like my smile had frozen. Dude was so sexy to me and I was loving how he hadn't played the waiting game and jumped right on it by reaching out to me. I didn't want to get my hopes up but I was also going to enjoy myself seeing where the relationship might go.

Before I got in the shower I sent Blair a text letting her what time and where to meet me for lunch and the smile still hadn't disappeared from my face.

As I was pulling up to Beaumarchais on West 13th street I saw Blair about to walk inside. I blew the horn and she turned towards my direction and then quickly turned away probably thinking I was some nigga trying to holla. I blew my horn again but this time I rolled down the window because I knew she couldn't see me through the dark ass tint.

"Girl, what's up," she smiled.

"Just wanted to let you know I am here but I'll be inside in a few. So go 'head and get our table," I said needing to return a call before I went inside.

"Cool, see you in a little bit." I rolled the window back up and parked my car. I quickly dialed the number that was texted to me keeping the conversation short.

"Is everything straight on your end?" the person on the other end of the call asked.

"Super straight. I'll get with you tomorrow."

"That's all I needed to hear." The call went dead and I got out ready to stuff my face. When I stepped inside I immediately spotted Blair who already had a champagne glass in hand.

"Is that a Bellini?" I questioned as I sat down at the table.

"You already know. I was going to order you one but I wasn't sure if you were drinking or not."

"Stop playing! You already know how I get down. Where's our waiter or waitress so I can order me one."

"Here he comes now." When he got to our table I ordered my drink and food too because I was starving. Luckily Blair had already looked over the menu so she knew what she wanted too.

"So how is everything going with you?" I asked getting comfortable in my chair. "That bad." I stated as Blair rolled her eyes and then paused them while looking up to the ceiling, cradling her drink.

"Things definitely aren't good."

"Really? How can things be that bad when you got that fine ass man of yours and he chipped. If only I had those type of problems."

"Girl, if you only knew," Blair said solemnly shaking her head.

"Well damn, tell me."

"He's constantly reminding me that he has it all and I have nothing."

"Oh gosh, he's one of those types. I shoulda known he was too good to be true. I see we gon' need a few drinks for this fool."

"You so crazy, Diamond."

"I'm so serious. There's nothing worse than somebody making you feel like you ain't good enough. I remember dealing with that shit with Rico."

"Girl, I remember."

"So then why are you letting yourself get in that same type of relationship, because trust me it aint gonna get no better."

"If I can find success of my own then it will. Michael will have to respect me. Right now he just looks at me as some wannabe model slash actress but if I can become a legitimate star like a Tyler Blake..."

"Not to cut you off, but wasn't that bitch looking fierce last night."

"Hell yeah! If only I could have a small percentage of her career I would be on cloud nine."

"And you can. Blair, you have talent. I remember that play you did in Brooklyn last year."

"You talking about at that hole in the wall spot."

"It was a tad small, but you were still dope and I'm not just telling you that. I was pleasantly surprised at how great you did. I know you talked about wanting to be an actress but when I saw you actually perform I was impressed. So have you been going on auditions?"

"Not really. Once I started getting serious with Michael he made me feel like I was wasting my time even pursuing it."

"Do you want to be an actress? Is that your dream?"

"Yes, it is."

"Then fuck what Michael thinks. You're young, beautiful and talented. You only live once. Make Michael choke on his words."

"That's what I want to do but I need to get some gigs to get me some exposure. My agent kept telling me I needed to drum up some publicity for myself but how can you get publicity when you're not getting any work."

"It's all about who you know. Don't you always see those motherfuckers on the blogs walking the red carpet and they haven't had a gig in forever. Girl, please we just have to hook you up with the right person. Oh my fuckin' goodness, I just had the best idea."

"What?"

"My friend Kennedy. That chick I introduced you to last night who was able to get my table switched so I could sit next to you."

"Oh yeah, I remember her."

"She works for Darcy who is like the Queen Bitch of pr. She can make you a star."

"Darcy reps major people. She's not going to want to be bothered with me unless I pay her a shit load of money which I don't have."

"Let me just talk to Kennedy and see what I

can do. You have to be optimistic. Trust me, I'll find a way to work it out for you."

"You really are a diamond. You've always been such a sweetheart. Whether it works out or not with Darcy thank you for trying."

"Stop it! I've known you forever. I still remember you coming over and playing hopscotch in front of my grandmother's apartment building. I would do anything to help you make your dreams come true. Plus I know what it's like wanting the approval of a man. But I hate to break it to you, Blair, you're never going to get it from Michael. But I want to help you because I want you to at least show him that you can make it without him."

"That would be nice. But enough about my problems let's talk about you. I'm loving your new Escalade, so you got rid of your Benz?"

"Nope, I still have it but I needed a truck too."

"You got a sugar daddy that I don't know about or did you win the lottery! How the hell can you afford a Benz and a new truck?"

"I've been doing some investing. I'm a lot smarter than I look."

"No you've always been smart. You were a double threat, street smart and book smart. Remember you used to write some of my papers for me in high school and you would beat a bitches ass that would fuck with us."

"Oh yeah, how can I forget," we laughed.

"But I'm happy for you. Growing up I always thought it would be so nice to have a man take care of me but it's actually somewhat degrading. Michael pays my bills and has me on a monthly allowance like I'm his child. He doesn't even think I'm sophisticated enough to pick out my own clothes. So kudos to you for being able to buy your own shit, hopefully that will be me soon."

"It will and toast to that," I said clicking our champagne glasses together. "Wait, before I forget, I need you to do something for me."

"Really? What could you possibly need from me?"

"Double date. I know you have a man so we don't have to call it a date for you. How about you be my escort."

"Who is it with?"

"Cameron and Kirk."

"Those basketball players we met last night?"

"Yes. He called me today and I told him I was meeting you and he suggested we all do dinner. Of course I accepted because I knew you wouldn't let me down," I grinned.

"Of course I can't let you down, although that Kirk seems a little full of himself but he is an NBA player what should I expect."

"Well he seems to be very interested in you."

"What I'm supposed to jump from one asshole to another. I think I'll stick with the one I got."

"Listen, I'm not asking you to become his baby mamma. Just do me a favor and go with me to dinner tonight."

"No problem. Michael already told me he was going to be busy tonight so I'm free."

"Great! Let's eat our lunch and get out of here. I want to take my time getting ready tonight because unlike you I think I might want to be Cameron's baby mamma," I laughed out loud.

"Diamond...Diamond...Diamond, what am I going to do with you!"

Kennedy

It was a surprisingly rather mild Saturday afternoon but instead of being out and about enjoying the sunny weather I was on my way to work. I was still tired from last night's event but none of that mattered because Darcy needed me to start working on our next big project. Darcy would always say that in her line of work all the days just ran together. There was no separation between the weekday and the weekends. Plus I was looking forward to going to work, because Darcy had already said my commission check was there waiting for me to pick it up and boy did I need that money. Living in New York City was kicking my ass. At first I was living in Queens but the hours I kept at work was making it painfully difficult to do the commute. When I spoke to Darcy about changing my hours she suggested I get out of Queens and move to the city. So I was now living in an apartment the size of a closet and the rent was basically eating up my entire paycheck. But this commission would have me sitting pretty for a minute. It also motivated me to go out and secure other deals for Darcy to keep the money rolling in.

As I was getting off the train and heading towards my job I heard my cell ringing and saw Diamond's name on the screen. "Hey, what's up, did you have a good time at the event last night?"

"I sure did! And I met me a cutie which made it even better."

"Of course you did. I wouldn't expect anything less," I said laughing. And I wouldn't. Diamond was a guy magnet. She revamped her entire look a year after having her baby and it was working wonders for her. Before she was a cute, sweet looking girl, now she had that whole sex kitten thing going but still classy not trashy.

"I wish you could've hung out with us."

"Me too but I had to work my ass off for this event. Because I brought the contact to Darcy I got a commission so I had to make sure everything went perfect."

"Well you did a great job because that was one of the best if not best events I had ever been to. You should pat yourself on the back."

"Girl stop...but I did do my thing though," we both laughed.

"But listen, I wanted to speak to you about something else."

"What's up?"

"Remember the girl I was with last night. The one you switched my seat around for so I could sit next to her."

"Oh yeah, she's dating that big entertainment lawyer."

"Exactly."

"What about her?"

"Well, we just finished having lunch and she said she really wants to break into the business."

"What does she do?"

"She's an actress and before you ask, no she hasn't had any major roles but she is extremely talented."

"So what do you want me to do?"

"She just needs some great exposure to create some buzz and get her noticed. Darcy is a huge publicist she could get her that exposure."

"Honestly, Darcy doesn't take on people who aren't known and if she does she charges them like five to ten thousand a month. Who's going to foot that bill?"

"I will."

"Excuse me, what did you say?"

"If you make sure Darcy gets her the exposure she needs then I'll pay for it."

"Why would you do that and more importantly where would you get the money?"

"Listen, I've known Blair since I was a little girl. She's had a tough life and her boyfriend isn't exactly helping her self-esteem but you know what she really is talented. I'm not just saying that because we're close friends it's the truth. If I can help her make it then I will."

"Wow, I hope she knows how lucky she is to have you do this for her. But I would recommend you make it a loan. Say she blows up which is very possible if we take her on as a client. When the checks start rolling in you should get your money back. I know Blair is your friend but this is also business."

"That's true but first let's see if you can get Darcy to do it."

"Oh, I promise you she'll do it and I'll make sure because when I bring on a client I get a commission."

"Great! That works out perfectly."

"Sure does. And trust it'll be me doing all the work, so I'll make sure you get your money's worth. I'll have Blair's name on the tip of every casting director's tongue."

"Kennedy that would be awesome."

"I'm actually on my way to the office right now and I'll discuss it with Darcy. So I should have good news for you shortly."

"Wow, it would be great if I had some good news for Blair when we meet for dinner tonight."

"I'm about hundred percent positive you will."

"I hope so but call me as soon as you know something."

"I will but Diamond make sure you really have the money because Darcy doesn't play when it comes to getting paid. She'll want a three-month retainer fee up front. So I'll try my hardest to get her to charge you the lower end but you'll still need at least fifteen thousand dollars."

"I tell you what, if she agrees she can get her money tonight?"

"Are you serious! Diamond, how are you going to get your hands on that type of money?"

"I had some money saved and hooked up with an investment company and the money has been rolling in ever since."

"I tell you what, when I get my hands on a couple of dollars I need that dude's number. I would use this commission check I'm about to get but I'm so behind on bills I need every dollar. But I have some other projects coming so hopefully soon. I mean damn if you can get your hands on fifteen stacks just like that then I need to be a part of whatever you got going on."

"Girl, you know I got you. But right now just focus on getting this thing done for Blair."

"Oh I can guarantee you, if you have fifteen thousand dollars to give Darcy tonight then she'll get to working for Blair asap...that I can promise you."

"Then I'll be waiting for your call."

When I hung up with Diamond this huge burst

of energy shot through me. I couldn't remember exactly what Blair looked like but I do recall when Diamond introduced us I thought she was very pretty and if she truly is talented then it would be so much fun to take an unknown and make her into a star. Because like I told Diamond, Darcy would no doubt put all the work on me but I was excited because this would be an opportunity to see if I could make magic from scratch. It also didn't hurt that I would have some more commission money coming in.

When I got to the office I went straight to Darcy's office and the door was half way opened and she was tonguing down some man. I guess they felt my presence because they stopped, exchanged a few words and came walking out. The man looked very familiar but I couldn't remember where I knew him from and I hated when that happened. As he made his exit he arrogantly walked past me. I guess with my baseball cap on and sweats he assumed I was just some low level help. Not letting his attitude distract me, I kept it moving straight to Darcy as I had important issues to discuss.

"Kennedy, I'm glad you were able to come in this afternoon as I have a ton of things for you to do."

"Not a problem but there is something I want to discuss with you first."

"If it's about the check..."

"Actually it wasn't but since you brought it up, what about the check?"

'There's been a slight problem and I won't be able to give you the commission for this project."

"Excuse me! When you called this morning asking me to come in you said my check was here waiting for me."

"At that time I thought it would be but some unexpected expenses came up and I'm not going to be able to do it."

"Darcy, I earned that commission and I need the money."

"We all need money, Kennedy, but things happen. You'll have plenty of opportunities to make commissions. The same way you brought me that project you'll bring me more."

I felt my left eye twitching, which happened when I was about to explode. I had put up with a lot of bullshit from Darcy but this was the final straw. It was taking all my strength not to snatch her by her weave and beat her ass. But instead I took a deep breath and calmed myself down. No matter how badly I wanted to use her petite frame to swing around the office like a baseball bat and demolish it, I let my good sense prevail. I was done working for Darcy but I wouldn't tell her I quit by coming for her neck instead I would keep it professional and submit my letter of resignation.

"You're right, things happen."

"I knew you would understand. Now what is it that you wanted to talk to me about?"

"Oh, it was nothing. I'll get started on the work you need for me to get done."

"Good you do that. No need to go over anything as you already know what to do and I'm running late for my spa treatment. Call me if you need me if I don't answer leave a message and I'll get back to you when I'm done."

I watched in disgust as Darcy sashayed out the office with her designer sunglasses, handbag and stilettos on. Her entire getup probably cost more than the money owed to me but she didn't care because as long as her pocket stayed full damn the rest of us. I couldn't get to my computer fast enough to type my letter of resignation. I would tell Darcy to go screw herself in the most polished way possible. As I was starting to type my letter I noticed a text message from Diamond. Instead of responding with a text I decided to give her the news with a phone call.

"Girl, sorry I bothered you but I was anxious to see what Darcy had to say," Diamond said unable to contain her enthusiasm.

"I had to burst your bubble but I didn't get a chance to tell Darcy."

"So are you going to talk to her later on today? You know I want to get this ball rolling."

"No, if you want to use Darcy's services you'll have to reach out to her yourself because I'm quitting...today."

"What! Why?"

"You know that commission check I was anxious to get she said some unexpected expenses came up and she can't give it to me. I bust my ass everyday for that chick and that's the thanks I get. I'm fed the fuck up. I can go to a bunch of other PR firms and work for them. It may not be all glitz and glam like doing entertainment PR but at least I'll make way more money and have much better working hours. I've had enough of dealing with Darcy and her bullshit."

"That's so fucked up. Every time I want us to hangout you can't because you're doing something for her so I know how hard you work. Damn, Kennedy, I hate this had to happen, I was so excited."

"I know, I was too but I can't keep busting my ass for peanuts. At some point I have to draw the line and this is it."

"What if you didn't have to bust your ass for peanuts anymore?"

"I'm not! That's why I'm quitting...hello!"

"I meant not quit and not bust your ass for peanuts."

"I'm not following you."

"You keep working for Darcy but you do Blair's project on the side and I'll pay you the money I was going to pay Darcy instead. You already said it would be you handling the project anyway."

"Wait, you might be on to something. Use all

the connects and relationships I have from working here and let Blair benefit from them. She can walk all the red carpets at the events we do and I can get her invitations to other stuff we do all the time. I can also make sure Blair is on the list so she has the opportunity to meet the right people."

"Exactly! Blair can be the unofficial client but still get all the perks and instead of Darcy benefiting from all your hard work, you will."

"You are so smart and manipulative, Diamond and I love it! No wonder you're making all that money!"

"Ha!! I'll take that as a compliment. So is it a deal?"

"Yes, it's a deal! When do you want me to get started?"

"Right away. I don't know what your commission check was supposed to be but I think this will make up for it. So stop by my place and get your money."

"Are you serious?"

"I was going to give it to Darcy so why can't I give it to you. You're the one doing the work so I'm going to pay you for your services."

"I appreciate that but I'm not going to charge you what Darcy would. I'll do it for twenty-five hundred a month but I promise I'll bust my ass and make sure Blair gets her shine."

"Are you sure, Kennedy? I really don't mind

giving you the fifteen thousand and I know you need it. What you're about to do for Blair could change her life."

"I wouldn't feel comfortable charging you five thousand dollars a month. But you're right; I do need the money so the fifteen thousand will be for six months of services instead of three months. How does that sound?"

"Sounds fair to me."

"Awesome! I'll see you soon."

When I hung up with Diamond I twirled around in my chair kicking my legs and waving my arms. I couldn't believe this opportunity had fallen in my lap. Diamond came up with a win-win situation for me and this was just the beginning. I would do everything humanly possible to blow Blair up and use it to get more clients and eventually start my own PR Company. But unlike Darcy I would treat my employee's right. The break I'd been waiting for had finally come and I was ready.

Blair

When I arrived at the restaurant to meet Diamond I was nervous for some reason. Maybe because I knew I was late and she had already sent me two text messages letting me know they were waiting on me. I had every intention being on time but between arguing with Michael then trying to find something to wear the time got away. The hostess walked me to their table and everyone seemed to be in a good mood.

"I hope whatever you all are laughing about has nothing to do with me," I smiled.

"You finally made it," Diamond grinned, standing up to give me a hug.

"Sorry I'm late."

"You're here now that's all that matters."

"She's right," Kirk said before standing up and pulling out my chair so I could sit down. I wasn't expecting that and it almost made me feel uncomfortable.

"Thank you." He simply smiled and sat back down. "So did you guys already order?"

"No, Kirk insisted we wait on you. He said it would be rude not to. That's why I was blowing your phone up making sure you were coming."

"Aren't you the gentleman," I stated looking over at Kirk. I was being partly sarcastic but I was still trying to figure out if he was really a gentleman or running game.

"I only did what I'd want you to do if the situation was reversed. You would wait for me wouldn't you?"

"He sounded so sure that I found myself saying, "Yes, of course I would."

"That's what I thought."

"Now that we got that out the way let's order because I'm ready to eat."

"Diamond, you're always ready to eat," I laughed.

"Yeah, didn't the two of you have lunch today."

"True, but Cameron, do you know how many hours ago that was. I mean you never heard of breakfast, lunch and dinner. I need all my meals plus snacks."

"Nothing wrong with that. I like a woman with a healthy appetite," Cameron beamed, reaching over and squeezing Diamond's thigh. She laughed and kissed his cheek. Then he nuzzled her nose and they tickled each other like little kids. I looked at them baffled for a moment because instead of acting like they just met last night it seemed they knew each other forever.

"I think Cameron finally met a woman who is just as playful as him," Kirk commented while Diamond and Cameron seemed to be in their own little world.

"Yeah, they seem to have instantly clicked."

"You mean unlike us."

"That's not what I said."

"But it's what you were thinking."

"No, I was thinking it's nice to see a guy put such a huge smile on Diamond's face. She's such a sweetheart and deserves it."

"If you give me a chance I can make you smile like that too."

"I told you last night that I'm in a relationship."

"Maybe, but he sure doesn't have you smiling like that."

"I glanced over at Diamond and Cameron and he was right. Even in the best of times Michael never made my face light up the way Diamond's was.

"I'm extremely happy in my relationship... thank you very much."

"If that true, I'm happy for you."

"What about you? Is your girlfriend happy with you?" Kirk paused for a moment and laughed.

"My girlfriend broke up with me about a year ago, so that would be a no."

"Why did she break up with you?"

"She said I never made time for her. I kept saying I would but never did. Then one day I realized I never made time for her because I didn't really enjoy being around her. But it was easier to stay with her because it wasn't like she was keeping me from doing what I wanted to do. Eventually she got tired of it and bounced. I didn't try to stop her because it was the best thing for both of us."

"Interesting."

"So if your man is making you happy, Blair, that's a beautiful thing but if he's not, maybe you should consider other options."

"One of those options being you?"

"I don't consider myself exactly a bad catch. But seriously, I don't know what would happen between us. We might realize we can't stand each other or we might fall in love, would it hurt to see?"

"Is everyone ready to order?" the waiter asked snapping all of us out of our conversations.

"Excuse me, I have to take this call. Diamond, order me whatever you get. I'll be right back." I walked towards the back of the restaurant trying to find a somewhat quiet location. "Hey, how are you?"

"I'm fine. Where are you?"

"I went to dinner with Diamond."

"You didn't tell me you were going out."

"If you hadn't hung up on me earlier I would have."

"Blair, what you were talking about was irrelevant

and I was tired of the bickering so I hung up."

"Discussing my feelings and my career isn't irrelevant."

"What career, you don't have one."

"The career that I want to have."

"Anyway, how long are you going to be out with your friend."

"Her name is Diamond and I'm not sure."

"Go home after dinner and I'll see you later."

"But..." before I could say another word I realized Michael had ended the call. I wanted to cry, throw my phone and scream but instead I walked back to the table. I noticed a few people getting autographs from Kirk and he graciously signed them. But no matter how nice he seemed to be, I kept feeling he was an asshole just like Michael and it would only be a matter of time before his true colors showed.

"Is everything ok?" Diamond asked when I sat back down.

"I'm fine," I lied.

"I was telling Cameron and Kirk that the same way people were coming up to them asking for their autographs that soon people will be doing it to you."

"Huh...what are you talking about?"

"I told you I was on it. My girl who did that event we all attended last night has agreed to do PR for you."

"Are you serious?"

"Yep, I was going to tell you the good news later but you came back to the table with a look of death on your face and I wanted to make you smile."

"I've been trying to get her to let me do the same thing," When Kirk said that I couldn't help but look at him with a smirk.

"You better snatch her up while you can because soon you'll need an appointment just to get her on the phone."

"So what is it that you do?"

"Don't pay Diamond any attention," I said, trying to brush Kirk off.

"She can't be just making the shit up. What do you do?"

"Nothing really."

"Ok, let me rephrase the question. What do you want to do that requires you to need a publicist?"

"I want a career as an actress so I'm hoping a publicist will get me the right exposure."

"If that's what you want then you should go for it."

"You don't think I sound stupid?"

"Why would I think that?"

"This is New York. I'm sure you meet hundreds of girls who all say they want to be an actress."

"No, they mostly say they are models. But it doesn't matter because they're not you. If you want to be an actress and you're willing to put in the work to make it happen then you should give it your all.

I remember growing up when I would tell people I wanted to play in the NBA they would clown me and say it would never happen. My first year in the league I was named Rookie Of The Year, I have a huge Nike endorsement and I'm the star player for the New York Knicks. If I'd listened to all those people who clowned me none of that would've happened. So never let someone kill your dreams if you're willing to put in the work to make it happen."

"Thank you for sharing that with me."

"See that, I was able to put a smile on your face."

"Finally, our food is here, let's eat," I heard Diamond say. Our dinner arrived right on time. I welcomed the diversion because Kirk was starting to make me feel a certain kind of way. With his six-foot-four inch muscular frame, dark eyes and chiseled model face it would be easy to find Kirk physically attractive but me thinking he would behave like the typical arrogant athlete made him almost repulsive to me. But I was starting to believe my preconceived notion of him was wrong and that scared me. I was already dealing with having a fucked up relationship with Michael and bringing Kirk in the mix would just make shit even more complicated. So I decided to eat my food and limit my conversation with Kirk for the rest of the night.

"You didn't have to take me home, but thank you," I said to Kirk when we pulled up to the front of my apartment on Central Park West.

"I wanted to. You seemed to be ignoring me throughout dinner and I figured this might be my last chance to plead my case."

"Plead your case...and what case would that be?"

"You already know. I think you're just trying to be difficult but so you know I'm not giving up." He gave me a half smile that made him even sexier.

"Kirk, I'm flattered that you're interested in me but it wouldn't work between us."

"Cut it out, Kennedy. How would you know if you're not willing to give it a try?"

"I don't want to try."

"Really?" he asked with a raised eyebrow. "I don't believe you."

"It doesn't matter what you believe. Again, thanks for the ride home." As I was opening the door to exit, Kirk reached over and grabbed my arm. "What is it?"

"Here," he said handing me a piece of paper. "Take my number, in case you change your mind."

"I won't."

"Just take it," he insisted. I took the paper and put it in my purse. We made eye contact one last time before I told him goodnight and stepped out his car. I didn't look back but I could feel him staring at me as I went inside my building. The doorman was holding the door for me as I walked up. I could see he was trying to figure out who was the driver of the four-door cocaine white Bentley I just got out of. I was about to tell him to stop being nosey but kept it moving to the elevator. On my way up I opened up my purse and opened up the paper that had Kirk's number on it. I knew I should ball it up and throw it away but something held me back. I folded the paper back up and put it in my purse.

As I walked down the hallway to my apartment I kept thinking about Kirk's smile and the last words he said to me. He seemed so genuine but then again from my experience all men started off that way but once they got you they got brand new. *Forget Kirk McKnight. The only thing I need to concentrate on is getting my life together and having a career. I can't be just the girlfriend of Michael Frost forever,* I thought to myself as I opened the door to go inside my apartment. When I tossed my purse and keys down on the table and turned on the light I was startled to see Michael sitting on the couch.

"What are you doing here?"

"How was your dinner?" It was typical Michael to ignore my question and ask me one instead.

"It was fine."

"It takes you two-and-a-half-hours to eat," he said looking at his watch.

"We were talking."

"We, were there other people with you?"

"No, just Diamond but we had a lot to catch up on." My first instinct was to lie even though technically I hadn't done anything wrong but I knew Michael wouldn't see it like that.

"Did you have a good time?"

"It was just dinner but I always enjoy Diamond's company."

"I see you wore my favorite dress," he stated before standing up and walking towards me. I had forgotten that after we argued and he hung up on me I purposely put on the ruby red cocktail dress to spite him in my own twisted way.

"You must've known you would see me tonight because you know what this dress does to me," he said, as he used one hand to unzip my dress and the other to slide his hand up my thigh. He then slid my thong to the side before inserting his finger inside of me. "Damn, your pussy is so wet," he whispered in my ear before cupping my breast and licking my hardened nipple as I begged him to fuck me.

I lifted my leg up and wrapped it around his waist as he finger fucked me and sprinkled my neck with kisses. "Oh, that feels so good," I moaned.

"Do you want this dick?"

"Yes, I do..." I said, breathlessly.

"You sure?" he asked pulling my hair and turning my face towards his. His eyes always seemed to hypnotize me and I jerked my mouth towards his yearning for our lips to connect but he stopped me.

"Don't you want me?" my voice was full of uncertainty.

"Of course I do but I want you to do something for me first." I was confused but then he slid out his finger and put it to my mouth. "I want you to know what I taste when my tongue is inside of you." He caressed his finger across my bottom lip until gradually prying them open. He massaged his finger in and out of my mouth as if I was giving him a blowjob. Before I knew it Michael had me sprawled across the couch and his dick was deep inside of me. It felt so good I accidently bit down on his finger but that seemed to turn him on even more as each thrust became more intense.

As usual all the anger and resentment I was feeling towards Michael disappeared—at least for the moment. All I wanted to do was get caught up in the rapture of my man being inside of me, loving me and holding me. My mind and body had become an addict for what Michael gave me and I willingly took each dose.

Diamond

I was tossing and turning thinking about my night with Cameron. When he dropped me off it took all my strength not to invite him in. The only reason I didn't was because I knew we would fuck. I had it bad for the boy but I knew it wasn't time to give up the goods just yet. I mean it was our first date and I honestly wanted him to be a keeper, so I couldn't give into temptation—at least not yet.

My body slithered across the silk sheets as I let my mind begin imagining what could've happened between me and Cameron tonight, if I hadn't pressed the brake. Right as the dream was getting good it got disrupted by a nightmare or was it my reality?

"Bitch, where yo' motherfuckin' stash at!" If it wasn't for the cold steel pressed against my temple I would've sworn this shit had somehow accidentally got mixed up in my dream. But all doubt went out the door when the masked assailant jammed the gun against my forehead so hard it hit the back of the bedpost.

"Who are you and what the fuck do you want from me?" I mumbled quickly awakening from my sleep and praying this motherfucker wasn't here to rape me.

"Bitch, you know what I want!"

"Please don't rape me. I'm begging you," I pleaded holding the covers tightly over my body.

"I don't want yo' pussy."

"Then what?" my voice was trembling while my eyes darted around the room trying to see what I could use as a weapon.

"I want your money and your drugs, Bitch!" I swallowed hard as that wasn't the response I was expecting.

"I don't know what you talkin' 'bout! Why would I have drugs in my house...I don't fuck wit' that shit! All I got is two hundred dollars in my wallet and you can take it!"

"Yo' lying ass! Bitch, I know who the fuck you are. You moving more keys then most niggas out here so if you wanna stay alive you better come up with that cash and stash or you can start requesting yo' last rites."

"I don't know what the fuck you talkin' 'bout...I swear! Ain't no drugs up in here." Next thing I know this nigga pistol whip me with his gun. I could feel the open gash and I put my hand over it trying to stop the blood but it continued to trickle down.

"Now do you understand I ain't playin' wit yo' dumbass!"

"I don't have any drugs here but I do have some money," I admitted as I pressed down on my head hoping the pain would stop.

"You bet not be lyin.'"

"I'm not...I promise."

"Where the money at?"

"In that closet inside the black duffel bag on the top shelf." At this point only two things were on my mind. I was thankful Destiny was with her dad so she didn't have to be a witness to this bullshit and staying alive.

"Yo, it's 'bout a hundred g's in here! Yeah, Bitch I'll let you live," he continued. Even through the mask I could tell the nigga was cheesing and shit. I thought he was about to break out and do a happy dance. "Next time I come back you betta have some drugs too," he warned but almost in a joking type way. At this point I didn't even care I just wanted him out of my crib.

"You got yo' money and could you just go!"

"Calm yo' ass down. I got what I wanted. I'm outta here." That nigga pimp walked out my bedroom like he had just hit the jackpot and I guess to him he did. But luckily for me it was only a small percentage of what I really had. Don't get it twisted I was pissed that this nigga had the audacity to break into my crib, put a gun to my head and steal my money, but what could I do.

I fucked up and I had no one to blame but myself. I had been saying I needed to move into a doorman building but I loved my spacious renovated two-bedroom apartment in Harlem. Never did I feel I wasn't safe because I didn't think anybody knew I pushed drugs. Yeah I had the cars, jewelry and clothes but I kept my shit low key and felt I stayed under the radar but unfortunately I was wrong. I figured a few nosey people in my neighborhood thought I was selling pussy or was some king pin's bottom bitch but never that I was *that bitch* who was a major distributor to mostly all the street pushers.

Somehow though the streets got to talking and my secret was out. All I could do now was regroup, change shit up and be thankful that my mistakes didn't cost me my life. The first thing I planned on doing was moving ASAP. The next thing was purchase a gun for protection. Because best believe the person who attacked me, would start running his mouth letting motherfuckers know he made a come up off me, and other thirsty niggas would now try to do the same thing.

I didn't even feel safe staying in my apartment for the rest of the night. I grabbed my luggage and started packing shit up. I threw everything I could in my bags before I got dressed. I decided I would stay with my mom until I could come back and get the rest of my stuff.

Before I left I went in the bathroom and looked at the gash on my head. It didn't look as bad as it felt which I was grateful about. I cleaned it before putting a bandage on it and I started trying to figure out what lie I would tell my mother to explain it away. This wasn't the life I expected when I got into the game but I should've known that shit wouldn't stay rosy forever. Another lesson learned. With all the easy money that came from hustling you better be prepared to accept the bad.

The first thing I did when I woke up was reach in my bag for some Excedrin Migraine. My head was still throbbing from that pop I took on the head.

"Diamond, what are you doing here," my mom asked when she saw me standing in the kitchen pouring myself a glass of water.

"I came last night. I didn't want to wake you up," I responded casually.

"What happened to your head?"

"Oh, it's nothing," I answered vaguely. My mother's facial expression was screaming concern so I was trying my best to play it cool.

"Let me see," she said, smoothing back my hair to lift up the bandage. "Did you go to the doctor? That cut looks painful."

"I'm fine," I insisted, moving away.

"Did you get in a fight?"

"No, I was in a car accident." That was the first lie that popped in my head so I ran with it.

"Did somebody hit you? I hope you called the police and filed a report."

"It was my fault. I was texting and hit something."

"How many times have I told you about driving and texting at the same time. You lucky all you got was a bump on your head," my mother pointed her finger scolding me.

"You're right, it was a dumb mistake. It'll never happen again."

"I hope not. If anything happened to you I don't know what I'd do."

"Nothing is going to happen to me. But I do need a favor."

"What kind of favor?" she asked with a quizzical look on her face.

"Can Destiny and I stay with you for awhile?"

"Of course! That ain't no favor. You know you always welcomed here. But what's wrong with your place."

"I've decided to move."

"Really? But you always tell me how much you love your apartment."

"I do...I meant I did but there has been several break-ins lately and I'm afraid for our safety. I want to move into a more secure building."

"I can't blame you for that. Times are tough

right now and the last thing you need is somebody breaking into your apartment and God forbid hurt you and Destiny. You stay here for as long as you like."

"Thanks, Mom, I really appreciate that."

"No need to thank me. So where is Destiny, she still sleeping?"

"No she's actually with Rico. He's bringing her back today." Right when I said his name I saw my phone vibrating and his name on the screen. "That's him now, let me get this."

"Take your call, I need to go get dressed anyway," my mom said, kissing me on my forehead before leaving the kitchen.

"Hello," I answered not in the mood to speak to Rico.

"I'm about to drop off Destiny...you home?"

"You can bring her to my mother's house."

"What, you at your mom's crib?"

"Yes, that's why I want you to bring Destiny here," I huffed.

"So what you stayed at your mom's house last night?"

"What's with all the questions?"

"I'm just asking."

"Well stop it. I'll be here when you drop Destiny off," I smacked then hung up the phone. I leaned on the kitchen counter wondering what was up with Rico's questions. Then I thought about me getting robbed last night and how convenient it was that Destiny wasn't home because she was with her father. *No, that motherfucker wouldn't have me set up or would he? He doesn't even know I'm supplying drugs to the streets or does he?* Man the questions were spinning around so fast in my head I was getting dizzy.

I went to sit down because the anger was building up and I had to calm myself down. It was no secret that Rico couldn't stand the fact that I dropped his whorish ass and moved on to become my own woman but could he hate me that much. I mean I was the mother of his child. Would he actually green light a nigga running up in my crib, stealing from me and smacking me upside the head with a gun? As much as Rico worked my nerves I didn't want to believe that but something in the water damn sure wasn't clean. I prayed that Rico had nothing to do with the robbery but if he did, everybody involved was going to wish they left me for dead.

Kennedy

"Kennedy, I need for you to go to that club in the Meat Packing District, it's called," she looked down and began fidgeting with some papers. "You know that club you wrote the proposal for."

"Oh, you're talking about The Double Seven."

"Yes, well they are anxious to read over it and I want you to personally deliver it to the owner, who is there right now."

"Don't you think it would leave a better impression if you went and delivered it yourself?"

"No of course not. I'm a celebrity myself. It's expected that I don't have time to do such trivial things…that's what I have you for. Here's the address," Darcy said, handing me a card. "Now hurry along. If we get them for a client it would be huge. They're one of the hottest nightclubs right now and with this being New York who knows how long that will last."

"I'm sure that's what they want to hire us for…

to make it last."

"That's what we're here for to sell them the dream and as long as they're willing to pay for it all is well. Now handle that and get back because I have some other projects for you to work on."

It was moments like this I regretted not handing in my resignation but I was fifteen thousand richer because of it so how could I really complain.

When the cab dropped me off on Ganesvoort Street, I was surprised to see a filming crew and buses in front of the club. People were standing around as if they were on some type of break from shooting. I went inside and saw a tall, blonde rocker looking dude standing behind the bar and hoped he could be of some assistance.

"Hi, can you tell me where the owner is. I have some papers I need to give him."

"He should be here in the next ten minutes or so. You can have a seat and wait for him."

"Thanks, I'll do that."

"Would you like a drink or anything while you wait?"

"No, I'm good but thanks but umm what are they shooting in here?"

"Some hip hop video. I don't listen to that music but from the big hoopla they're making he's suppose to be a big time artist," he responded nonchalantly, while continuing to set up the bar.

"Why is everybody standing around, are they on some type of break?"

"From what I was told some girl got injured."

"Injured?"

"Yeah, that lady over there," I peered over in the direction he was pointing. "She told me because she wanted to know if we had a first aid kit.'"

When I realized I recognized the lady he was pointing at I stood up from the bar stool and headed in her direction.

"Tish, hi! It's good to see you," I smiled, giving her a hug.

"Kennedy, it's always good to see you! I heard the event was spectacular. Thanks so much for the invite. I was so mad I couldn't attend but I was stuck in LA."

"I understand...you're a busy girl. So what do you have going on here today?"

"We're shooting a music video for Skee Patron."

"Nice...."

"Yeah but the leading lady fell and we think she broke her ankle and she has some scratches on her legs and arm. I mean what model doesn't know how to run in heels...what a nightmare!"

"So what are you going to do?"

"I've been on the phone for the last thirty minutes trying to replace her dumbass. But it's so last minute nobody is available. This video is already over budget and if we waste anymore time the label is going to freak. This is my biggest video yet, I don't want to fuck things up."

"Tish, I have the perfect girl for you."

"You do?" she asked as if in shock.

"Yes! We have a new client she would be perfect."

"Is she a model?"

"An actress, which is even better because she has the looks plus the acting skills."

"What's her name?"

"Blair."

"I've never heard of her, what movies has she stared in?"

"She's still under the radar because the movies that she's staring in haven't been released yet. She has a role in the Tyler Perry movie that's coming out at the end of the year and she's in the running for lead in the next Tarantino movie. This girl is going to be huge. And what's great for you is that she's not the standard video girl that everybody has seen. This will be her first one."

"Really." Her eyes gleamed in anticipation of getting her hands on some fresh new meat. "I know if Darcy took her on as a client she must be hot. How fast can she get here?"

"I'll get her on the phone now." I hurried off to a corner with my fingers crossed that Blair would answer her phone. It rang and rang and rang then it went to voicemail. So I hung up and called her again. "Dammit Blair, answer the fuckin' phone," I yelled in a whispering voice so no one else could hear how frustrated I was.

"Hello." I groggy female voice answered the phone and I assumed it had to be Blair.

"Blair, wake up!"

"Who is this?" I could tell she was still half asleep.

"It's Kennedy."

"Who?"

"Your publicist."

"Oh, Kennedy...hi," she said, with her voice perking up.

"I need you to get up and come to 63 Ganesvoort Street...now."

"Why, what's going on there?"

"You're going to be the leading lady for Skee Patron's new video."

"Seriously...you got me a job already in a Skee Patron video and I'm the lead."

"Yes and yes but only if you can get out the bed and get here now."

"I'm coming," she stuttered.

"Wait, you do know how to run in heels don't you?"

"Yeah, why?"

"Only checking, because you will be doing

some running. And Blair, fix yourself up. I know you're just waking up but I don't want you coming down here looking like it."

"I got you and trust me I know how to do the get ready quick look."

"Great, see you shortly."

"Were you able to get in touch with her because if not, I just got the call that Jourdan Dunn is in town and would love to do it?"

"No need! I just got off the phone with Blair and she's on the way. Trust me, Tish, you'll love her."

"I'll call the office and let them know we have our model."

"You do that." While Tish made her phone call I noticed the bartender waving his hand to get my attention. He then pointed his finger towards the door and I noticed a middle age Italian looking man coming in. I figured that was the owner. I smiled and gave the bartender thumbs up before placing my own call.

"Are you on your way back?" Darcy wanted to know before I even had a chance to say hello.

"Actually, I'm still waiting for the owner. They not sure when he'll get here. But I can leave the papers with the bartender so I can get back to the office," I suggested, knowing damn well that wouldn't fly over with Darcy.

"Oh please, you might as well dump it in the trash in that case. Just stay there for however long it takes until you can personally give the paper to the owner. Your work will be here waiting for you when you get back. Gotta go...bye."

Now that I took care of Darcy all I had to worry about was Blair. I was keeping my fingers crossed that she wouldn't let me down. I looked at the time on my watch while drumming my fingers on the table. This was her first test and it was up to Blair whether she would pass or fail.

Blair

After getting off the phone with Kennedy, I literally took a shower and got dressed in fifteen minutes. Obviously Kennedy was on top of her job and I wasn't about to let her down. I would've been ready quicker but I debated on what I should wear. I knew whoever the stylist was on set would provide wardrobe but I still wanted to make the right first impression. I opted on some form fitting jeans and a white V-neck t-shirt and some black sling back heels. I word my diamond stud earrings and my hair pulled up in a loose ponytail. As I gave myself a final glance over in the full-length mirror I felt this gave me the perfect understated yet sexy appeal. I grabbed my purse and keys and headed out the door.

"Good afternoon, Miss Blair," my doorman greeted me when I got off the elevator downstairs.

"Good afternoon to you too," I smiled, brushing past him in a hurry.

"Someone is waiting for you," he said admiringly.

"He's been out there for awhile. He must think you're some kind of special."

I didn't know what my doorman was talking about until I walked outside and saw Kirk parked in front of my building in his white Bentley. "Please don't think I'm a crazy stalker I just had to see you again. I wasn't confident you would put my phone number to use so I came to you," Kirk admitted when he got out his car.

"I don't know what to say."

"Say you'll let me take you to lunch."

"I would...I mean I can't..."

"Which one is it?" he asked cutting me off with his signature half smile.

"I meant I would but I can't because I have to go to work and I'm already running late."

"Then let me give you a ride."

"No you don't have to."

"Do we have to go through this all over again? I've been sitting out here for over an hour the least you can do is let me give you a ride."

"I can't believe you've been out here for that long. Don't you have a game, practice...something?"

"I had practice this morning and afterwards I came straight over here. I wasn't sure if I would miss you but you don't seem like you get up early in the morning so I was willing to take my chances."

"I guess it worked out for you."

"Only if you let me give you a ride."

"Fine," I laughed. There was no denying I was flattered by his attention and he was so cute doing it.

"Yes," he responded by pumping his fist in the air before opening the passenger door for me. "So where are we headed?"

"63 Ganesvoort."

"That's in the Meat Packing District...right?"

"That's right."

"You said you're going to work, so you have another job besides pursuing your acting career?"

"Actually, that publicist Diamond was talking about she got me the job."

"Damn, she's fast."

"I know. She called me at the last minute and I was so surprised."

"So what are you going to be doing?"

"I'm supposed to be the lead in Skee Patron's new video."

"Congratulations. That's a good look for you."

"Yeah, it's totally unexpected. One minute I'm trying to figure out how I can get myself some exposure the next I'm booked as the lead in the video for the biggest artist in hip hop. It's amazing what a great publicist can do."

"That is very true. You get the right team, ain't no telling how far you can go. And I think you can go far, Blair."

"You're gonna make me blush."

"That's a good thing."

"But seriously, I love how supportive you are."

"Everybody needs support. I don't care how successful you become."

"What about you...you're clearly on top of your game. I doubt you need any support."

"Yes I do. The higher you go the more support you need but it's a different kind of support."

"What do you mean?"

"Everybody knows who you are so it's important to align yourself with people who really believe in you and not just jumping on the train 'cause you already winning."

"Well I know you're busy but it would mean a lot to me if you stayed during the video shoot...you know and be my support."

"I would love to." I locked eyes with Kirk for a moment before glancing out the window and noticing we had pulled up in front of The Double Seven. All eyes seemed to be on us as we got out the car.

"That is some way to make an entrance. I'm Kennedy, in case you don't remember."

"I do, hi!"

"You look great and you look even better stepping out the Bentley with Kirk McKnight. I thought the attorney guy was your man I had no idea you were dating Kirk."

"We're just friends," I said, turning around

looking for him but he was already surrounded by a group of fans wanting autographs.

"This is every publicist dream. The media would eat this up. Do you know how much publicity you would get dating Kirk McKnight. This is perfect!"

"Listen, he is just my friend. Michael is my man. Got it?"

"Tish, over here," Kennedy waved at some woman totally ignoring what I said. "Tish this is Blair, the actress I was telling you about."

"Yeah, I just saw you get out the car with Kirk McKnight. Are you two dating?"

"N…"

"Yes, they are," Kennedy answered cutting me off. I could not believe she told a bold face lie in front of me after I had just told her we were only friends.

"Wow, this is great. Maybe we can find a way to get Kirk to do a cameo in the video. No, Skee would never go for it; he wants to be the only star. But that's okay we'll get them to take some pictures together. Kennedy, booking her was genius," the woman commented after it seemed for a second she was having a conversation with herself.

"I told you to trust me."

"Hold on one sec, Blair. Let me go speak to someone quickly and then I'll get you to hair and makeup."

"She'll be right here waiting for you, Tish. Take your time."

"Why did you lie to her about Kirk."

"Umm...is that all you have to say to me? What happened to thank you so fuckin' much Kennedy for getting me a dream gig?"

"You're right...thank you but..."

"No buts....K! You said you wanted to be a star. You've been frolicking around New York for how long and accomplished what? You think I got you the leading lady spot in a Skee Patron video by telling Tish the only stage you've been on is some hole in the wall in Brooklyn? No. I lied and I will continue to lie if it means getting my client the best gigs possible. If you don't believe in lying then you're in the wrong business. Magic doesn't happen by telling the truth."

"I get it."

"I hope so because when I took this project on my only intention was to make you a star. I'm trying to take you to the big leagues one gig at a time and it starts right here," Kennedy stated crisply, as she pointed her finger down towards the sidewalk cement. "I know you're a kept woman, but unless you plan on making that a full time career, no more waking up in the middle of the afternoon until your name can open up a movie. When I call, you should be up and ready, not sleeping your day away. We're in a business where opportunities only knock once. So I advise you to get your priorities straight because I'm in it to win."

"So am I."

"Then you better start acting like it," Kennedy said, bluntly before turning in her boots and walking away.

As I stood alone on the street I watched Kirk who was laughing signing autographs as fans continued to come up to him. Then I thought about Michael whose confidence was unshakable because he was the most sought after entertainment lawyer from the east to the west coast. Then there was me, always the underachiever. I didn't want to wake up twenty years from now and realize I wasted my life chasing behind men that had it all and I had absolutely nothing. So whatever Kennedy needed me to do, I would make it happen because there was no denying I wanted to be a Baller Bitch.

Diamond

When I heard the front doorbell ring, I took a deep breath before opening it. I knew it was Rico dropping off Destiny and I didn't want him to know that in my mind he was suspect number 1. I swallowed hard and opened the door.

"Hey, Rico," I said casually, as I reached out to get Destiny who was sleeping.

"What up. She still tired from all that birthday partying she did yesterday," he said, walking past me and laying Destiny down on the couch. I was tempted to say *Nigga, what the fuck is you doing, I didn't invite you in*, but because I needed to pick his brain I kept the slick shit to myself.

"I see," I gave a halfway smile before closing the door.

"So what you doing at your mom's house?"

"I spent the night."

"Word...why you do that?"

"Because somebody broke in my crib and

robbed me last night. That's why I got this knot on my head."

"What the fuck!" he belted and then quickly put his hand over his mouth, "Oh shit, I don't want to wake Destiny," he turned looking at her to make sure she was still asleep. His reaction and the shocked expression on his face almost made me believe he wasn't the culprit in this bullshit but I wasn't totally convinced. I knew from years of experience what a professional liar he could be.

"Yeah, he came in gun blazing."

"Did you see his face?"

"Nope, the punk ass nigga was masked up but I'll never forget his voice."

"Why would somebody target you to rob? It's not like you got money. Yeah, you pushing some nice whips and shit but I know it belong to some nigga you fuckin', it ain't like it's yours. That shit crazy," he continued shaking his head.

"As a matter of fact..." I wanted to burst this fool's bubble so bad but I caught myself.

"As a matter of fact what?" I wanted to be like *As a matter of fact them cars don't belong to no nigga they belong to me. I'm that bitch out here gettin' money and ain't* no *nigga giving me nada*. But that was out of the question because either Rico already knew that and was a very good actor or he didn't and there was no reason for me to start advertising the shit.

"As a matter of fact I was wondering the same thing. Why would anybody want to run up in my crib trying to rob me but they did. That's why I'm staying at my mother's place until I can find another spot."

"And don't go moving in wit' some nigga wit' my daughter. I ain't having that shit."

"Rico, I don't get down like that but if I did it wouldn't be none of your motherfuckin' business. I don't try to regulate who come in an out yo' crib so don't try that shit wit' me."

"First off, Destiny don't live wit' me she live wit' you. If she did live wit' me the only chick I would have around her was my main chick."

"And if I thought enough of a guy to move in with him then clearly he would be my man, not some random dude."

"It don't matter because the shit wouldn't last...you would work his nerves and he would toss yo' ass out and Destiny don't need to be caught up in all that bullshit."

"Rico, it's time for you to go," I popped, opening the door. I already had a headache from the pistol pop I got last night and now Rico was trying to make my shit explode.

"Don't get all pissy 'cause I'm speaking the truth."

"Dude, I'm already stressed enough. I refuse to let you get me riled up so take that mouth of yours and leave."

"See that's why yo' ass got robbed, 'cause you talk too much."

"Is that right...but you know what?"

"What?"

"I ain't worried. 'Cause best believe whoever is responsible for the shit is gon' regret they ever stepped foot in my crib. That I can promise you." I stared directly in Rico's eyes when I said that shit because it was like my warning to him. I wanted him to understand that if I found out he was involved baby daddy or not his ass was mine.

As I drove on my way to meet Cameron there was a mixture of excitement and nervousness bubbling in the pit of my stomach. I hadn't seen him since our dinner date with Blair and Kirk. After I was robbed later that night and was left with that gash decorating my forehead I didn't want to see Cameron until it had healed. I knew he would have started asking me a ton of questions and most I didn't have answers to. The ones I could answer I had no desire to make Cameron privy to that information. I started to imagine the horror on his face if I admitted that the self-employed entrepreneur I described myself to be was true, but my product of choice were illegal drugs. Nope, that wasn't going to happen.

Although I was still a romantic at heart even after all the hell Rico put me through, this was the first time I felt I had met a man that I could actually take seriously and have a meaningful relationship with. The majority of guys I dated after Rico were simply playthings to me. My heart had been so broken after Rico all I wanted to do was date dudes I could have fun with. I quickly found out that those types of men would show you a good time but it came with a lot of bullshit. They would wine and dine you, some would even lavish expensive gifts on me but at the end of the date they all expected those panties to drop. I found out the hard way that when shit seemed too sweet it's because it was.

I'll never forget the day a nigga I was dealing with took me on a shopping spree and afterwards he demanded I give him some head right there in the mall's parking lot. I hadn't even given him no pussy, I damn sure wasn't about to wrap my lips around his dick. I gave that motherfucker the deuces and told him he could keep his shit. I damn near got raped behind that fuckery and that's when I knew this wasn't the life for me. I wanted to live the good life but on my own terms, which eventually led me to a new game, called hustling. As I began to reminiscence about my introduction into becoming a major drug distributor, I realized that Cameron and I were pulling up to the restaurant at the exact same time. I noticed a big grin spread across his face when he saw me and I couldn't help but blush.

When I got out the car I wanted to run up to Cameron and give him a big hug and kiss but I hesitated wanting to stay cool, then I said fuck it. The moment he stepped out of his Range, I sprinted towards him like I was a little girl and he was Santa Claus holding all my toys for Christmas. "Baby, I missed you," I gushed, jumping into his arms.

"I missed you more," he said, holding me in front of him midair. His eyes spoke with such sincerity that I felt at that very moment I fell in love with him. "You better not ever stay away from me for that long again. Next time you go visit your family down south, I'm coming with you."

"I would love that," I smiled. I felt like a piece of shit for lying to Cameron but when I had to come up with an excuse for staying away that was the first lie that popped in my head. He didn't deserve to be lied to but I felt I had no choice. As we walked into the restaurant hand and hand guilt overcame me. There was a part of me that wanted to confess all my deep dark secrets but I held back. I did believe Cameron cared about me but I wasn't confident that it ran so deep he would forgive me for being so deceitful.

"So did you have a good time visiting your family?" Cameron asked when we sat down at our table.

"You should already know the answer to that

since we talked on the phone more than three times a day," I laughed.

"I know right. I know yo' people was like who is this crazy stalker you got calling your phone nonstop."

"No, they thought it was sweet and so did I."

"I couldn't help myself...I really did miss you. I was surprised just how much," he admitted in almost a shy way.

"Don't be embarrassed," I said, playfully rubbing the side of his face. "I missed you just as much. I was counting down the days I would be back home and back in your arms. You saw how fast I ran to you."

"I liked that...it was mad cute. I love that about you."

"Love what?"

"How open you are with your feelings. A lot of women try to play so high post, like they don't really care even if they do. But you, it's like you want me to know how much you care and I dig that."

"Cameron, I do care, you have no idea how much," I said caressing his hand.

"Stop that, you tryna make a nigga fall in love wit' you," he smirked.

"Only if you want to," I countered in a flirtatious voice.

"I think I do."

"Really?"

"Yep," he nodded. "So when are you going to let me come over and meet your daughter. Maybe the two of you can have me over for dinner," he laughed. What Cameron suggested caught me off guard so I sat there for a few seconds with a blank stare on my face.

"Is that a problem?" he asked with a raised eyebrow as he slid his hand away. "Don't tell me you're still fucking around with your daughter's father?"

"No, no, no, it's nothing like that," I quickly said wanting to assure him that wasn't the case. "It's been over with Rico for a very long time and I'm good with that...I put that on everything."

"So why when I made the suggestion to come over and meet your daughter you had this like scared look on your face?"

"I would love for you to meet Destiny it's just that right now I'm staying at my mom's crib so the whole come over for dinner thing isn't really good for me right now."

"Why are you staying at your mom's place?"

"There has been a lot of robberies in my building so I'm not feeling safe. I'm going to stay at my mom's until I can find another place, you know like a building with a doorman."

"Why didn't you tell me sooner? I can find you a place."

"You're so sweet. I appreciate that but I'm

good."

"Where are you trying to move?"

"I'm not sure if I'm going to stay uptown or move in the city or in Brooklyn or Queens. I haven't had an opportunity to start looking yet."

"Have you found a realtor yet?"

"No."

"You can use mine."

"But I'm not trying to buy a place."

"Nah, she does rental properties too, she does it all. Let me call her right now." Before I could say another word, Cameron was on his phone. Although I did appreciate him wanting to help me out I did not want some realtor that was cool with him all up in my business. She would need all sorts of paperwork, tax returns and I didn't have none of that shit. Because of my illegal dealings I had a certain way I moved that worked well for me and I didn't need nobody fucking that up.

"Damn, I don't need this shit," I mumbled under my breath, as my brain was scrambling trying to get my thoughts together.

"Just got off the phone with Marci, and she can meet with you tomorrow. I told her you were my special girl so she better give you top notch service."

"Baby, you didn't have to do that."

"I want to. You are my special girl."

"And that means so much to me but honestly I'm sure she's used to dealing with much bigger clients than me. She probably shows very expensive properties that are completely out of my price range. I don't want to waste her time."

"Don't worry about that. If you see something you like we'll work it out. I want you and your daughter to be safe. Plus, I have my own reasons for wanting you out your mother's place and having your own crib."

"Why?"

"Because I can't wait for you to have me over for dinner...I wanna see if you can cook." We both laughed before giving each other a kiss.

"You're a mess, you know that," I said rubbing the tip of my nose against his."

"How 'bout we're each other's messes."

"I like that," I smiled. And it was the truth I did like that. From the moment I met Cameron we clicked. It wasn't forced our chemistry came naturally. I had to figure out how to dead this situation with the realtor because Cameron was the real deal and I wasn't going to let anything fuck that up.

Kennedy

"Good morning," I beamed when I walked into the office.

"Good morning to you. You're in an awfully good mood," Tammy replied, with a look of bewilderment on her face. "Normally on the days I come in to intern, you're frowned up. It's nice to see you with a smile on your face."

"And it feels so good to have one. I think my days of coming to work with a frown on my face are behind me."

"Really! What gives? Did Darcy finally wise up and give you a promotion and a raise?"

"Nope. Let's just say I've found a way to give myself my own promotion and raise."

"Do tell," Tammy said as her eyes widened in anticipation. But before I could tell her, the queen of mean sashayed in.

"I'm glad you're both here. I just got a new client and you all have a lot of work to do."

"Who is it?"

"The fundraiser Tyler Blake hosted that I put together must have made a great impression."

You mean that I put together and never got my commission from I thought to myself as Darcy's self absorbed ass stood in front of us taking all the credit with a straight face.

"I'm sure it did," I said with slight sarcasm.

"But you know I never half ass anything so are we really surprised…but anyway…I've been hired to do the publicity for the new movie Tyler Blake is starring in."

"Wow, that's incredible!"

"Yeah, it really is," I chimed in.

"It's my first taste of that Hollywood money and I'm loving it. If I play my cards right this will be the first of many more movies to come."

"Then I guess you better get to work!" I said being extra cheerful.

"Yes we better. I know my best girl is going to kick ass on this project and of course you'll be rewarded properly."

"You mean like I was for the fundraiser I did?"

"Kennedy, let's go talk in my office for a moment," Darcy said, trying not to screw her face up in front of Tammy.

"Sure. Tammy, I'll be right back." I followed Darcy into her office and this entire situation was actually funny to me. The fact that Diamond had hit me off with the $15,000 to work Blair's PR services made Darcy's bullshit almost hilarious to me. Because trust, if I was still broke right now I would be ready to kick her ass.

"Close the door, Kennedy."

"Sure," I replied casually as if I had no idea she was pissed the fuck off right now.

"What was that in there," Darcy snapped, as she pointed her well-manicured finger to the left and rolled her slender neck.

"I don't understand."

"That comment you made about the fundraiser."

"Oh that. Well, it's true. You haven't given me my commission. Unless you have a check for me today."

"I explained that situation to you, Kennedy and you said you understood."

"Hmmm, I don't remember that part...you know understanding."

"Well I thought you did. And I don't appreciate you discussing that matter in front of the intern. It's inappropriate."

"I know what you mean about inappropriate." I could tell the slight grin I gave was about to send Darcy postal. It was like horns of the devil were rising from her head.

"Kennedy, I can understand that you are upset about the commission and I apologize." This shit right here was pure comedy. In all the time I worked for Darcy I had never ever heard her utter an apology to anybody not even her clients. And I knew she wasn't sincere it was called desperation.

"Well I appreciate your apology but it does nothing for my pockets." I could tell Darcy was surprised by my assertiveness but when you know your bills are paid and you got extra it's easy to be a little bold.

Darcy swallowed hard like she wanted to choke before she finally spoke. "If we do a great job on this project I'm expecting a nice check for our services. I tell you what; since I was unable to give you a commission for the fundraiser I'll give it to you for this instead. Of course that means I really need for you to kick ass."

"Don't I always."

"Yes, you do and maybe I don't tell you often enough but thank you for you're amazing contributions."

Wow, as thick as she's laying on this kiss up shit that check they cutting her must be astronomical I thought to myself.

"Well, I won't let you down."

"That's what I wanted to hear, Kennedy." Darcy's devil horns had now disappeared and her fake ass smile was now back in full effect. "I knew you wouldn't let me down."

The funny part was with all these compliments Darcy was bestowing upon me she had no intentions of giving me a dime in commission. She had burned me so many times that I could smell her bullshit coming from a mile away. Per usual, she would have me bust my ass doing all the work and not only would she take all the credit but when it was time to collect she would once again come up with some excuse as to why she had no money to give me. If Darcy had her way this same song and dance would last forever. She would be rich and thriving in her career while I would continue to be her broke slave but soon the joke would be on her. Darcy had no clue that the game had changed and I was now in the driver's seat.

I couldn't get to the W Hotel fast enough to meet Diamond for drinks. We had a ritual of meeting at the Whiskey Blue at least once a week to catch up on what was going on in our lives and today I was especially looking forward to it. By the time I got there the after work crowd was in full effect and Diamond was already on her first drink. She must've gotten there early since I was right on time.

"Girl, if you could've been a fly on the wall and heard my conversation with Darcy you would've fell out. It took all my strength not to fall out laughing at her and I owe it all to you," was the first thing out of my mouth before I even sat down on the barstool.

"Sit yo' ass down and tell me what the hell you

rambling on about," Diamond giggled.

"I was counting down every minute at work waiting to get off so I could tell you about my day."

"Why what happened?"

"What else...Darcy. She came in this morning bragging about getting a new gig and of course wanting to put all the work off on me. I called her out on not paying me my commission for our last major gig."

"Good for you!"

"Yeah, and of course she made her same empty promises but thanks to you putting me on I'm no longer fazed by Darcy. I'll forever be grateful to you for that."

"Girl, stop it. I came to you for the favor... remember. You were ready to give Darcy the middle finger and for good reason."

"True, but you came up with that brilliant idea and it worked out for all of us. That money you gave me has helped me out so much and it's also made me able to tolerate Darcy."

"To have to deal with her you deserve every penny. That woman is something else. But I know you can handle her. People like Darcy just prepare you to have the skills to go out there and win."

"And that's exactly what I plan to do," I smiled. "Okay, enough about that monster, what's going on with you? How was your trip to...where did you go again, North Carolina?"

"Yeah."

"I didn't even know you had family there."

"Yeah my aunt and a few cousins."

"Oh, so you had a good time?"

"It was cool. But I'm glad to be back home. You know there's nothing like New York and there's always something to do."

"You ain't lying and speaking of things to do. I put you on the list for Skee Patron's album release party. His record label is making it super exclusive so it should be really nice."

"Can't wait!"

"Oh, and it's a plus one."

"What! I can bring a guest. I really must be moving up."

"Shut up! But after that 15 stacks you gave me it's carte blanche for you!"

"I like the sound of that."

"So who are you going to bring?"

"Hopefully Cameron will want to come although he probably is already on the list."

"So wait, this thing with Cameron has turned into a full fledge love connection."

"What are you talking about? All I said was that I was inviting him to the party."

"But it's how you said it and the glazed look you had in your eyes while saying it."

"I didn't realize it was that obvious."

"Pretty much but I'm so happy for you! If

anybody deserves to find a great guy it's you."

"He is pretty awesome. Honestly these feelings I have for him have thrown me for a loop. Initially it was just being so physically attracted to him. That tall, lean muscular NBA body, with that smile, the dimples...fuck I'm getting all excited thinking about him now. But besides him being sexy as hell, he's so sweet and considerate. How can I be so lucky to find such a great guy?"

"Because you deserve it. You give off a tough exterior but you're the sweetest and most generous person I know. So instead of wondering how lucky you are, Cameron needs to be thinking about how lucky he is to have found you."

"Thank you for saying that, Kennedy."

"It's true. You've completely turned your life around for the better since you got rid of Rico's crazy ass. You've always been a wonderful mother to Destiny, but now you're clearly doing great financially with your investments, of course you're an incredible friend and now you've seemed to find love. Everything is working out for you and I couldn't be happier."

"Kennedy, stop it, you're going to make me tear up!"

"Fine, I'll stop. But I have a feeling both of our lives are about to go in an amazing direction and I can't wait!"

Blair

"How do you like it?" the beautician asked me as she turned my chair around to face the wide mirror. I stared at my reflection for what seemed like forever before I answered. It was different but not drastic which I liked. My semi makeover was Kennedy's idea and at first I was reluctant about changing my hair but she seemed to know what she was doing so I followed her advice.

"Kennedy said you would do a great job and she was right. I love it!"

"I always love a happy customer. Plus I do think the layers and highlights compliment your face and great bone structure."

"Thanks! And I'll definitely be back in a few weeks." I handed the beautician a tip before stopping at the receptionist to pay my enormous bill and heading out. Kennedy said she was one of the best in the business and had an extensive celebrity clientele list, her prices certainly reflected that. But I was trying to make it in the big leagues so I couldn't half ass on anything. And if the last couple of weeks were any indication of what I had to look forward to then I needed to be on point at all times.

Instead of getting in a cab I decided to take advantage of the beautiful day and walk home. Plus, I wanted to think about all the great things that had been happening for me, literally overnight and it was all thanks to Kennedy. It started at Skee Patron's video shoot...

2 Weeks Earlier...

When Kennedy walked away after giving me a stern warning about what it would take for me to make it as an actress, I stood on the sidewalk trying to sort out the different emotions I was feeling.

"Are you good?" I heard Kirk ask, shaking me out my thoughts.

"Honestly, I'm a little nervous...that's a lie. I'm extremely nervous."

"Relax, it's okay. I'm here as your support, remember."

"That's right," I gave a half smile. That means you can't leave me."

"I have no intentions of doing that. I'll be right by your side as long as you want me to. I promise."

"Blair, they're ready for you," Kennedy called out from a distance. She waved her hand for me to come on so I did and like Kirk promised he was right by my side.

"Tish said they are ready for you in hair and makeup, so follow me." As we were following Kennedy she stopped mid step. "Is he coming with you," she said pointing towards Kirk?

"Yeah, is that cool?"

"Sure, I think it's great. I'm just surprised since you said you all weren't dating." I could tell Kennedy was being sarcastic but I chose not to entertain it. I was already nervous and I didn't need any additional stress. I looked back at Kirk and he had a smirk on his face. I was relieved he found it all so humorous because it made me less tense.

"Your dressing room is right down there on the left," Tish said, meeting us at the entrance. *I have a dressing room!* Is what I wanted to say out loud but I knew Kennedy would want me to seem like a pro so I kept the fact that I was pleasantly surprised about that to myself.

"I have a few things to take care of so I'll let them do what they do but if you need me I'm only a phone call away," Kennedy informed me before making her exit.

"This is interesting. I've never been on a video set before. So this is what they do...throw a glam team on you, make you camera ready," Kirk joked.

"You know I really am glad you stayed. You're keeping me from having an anxiety attack."

"Don't be so nervous, you're in good hands. You got people doing your hair, makeup, dressing you, you can't go wrong. They'll probably carry you out to the set if you ask them to."

"Shut up. I'm glad you find this all so funny."

"Isn't that my job for the day, help you relax and stay calm."

"Yeah."

"How am I doing?"

"So far so good."

"If I do a really great job does that mean you'll let me take you out to dinner tonight so we can celebrate."

"Let me get through this video shoot first before we talk about celebrating anything."

"Listen, when you give me a job to do I always deliver. So I know you gon' nail this shit because I won't let you fail."

"You know what, I believe you."

"That's because you're a smart girl. Now sit back and enjoy the moment. This is only the beginning."

A calm came over me and I did exactly what Kirk suggested. For the next hour or so I let my glam squad turn me into a video vixen. But there would be no hoochie mama cheap looking outfits. The stylist had nothing but gorgeous gowns and high-end shoes, very classy but sexy outfits for me to wear. When they finished with me I barely recognized myself. Everything exemplified the word super, from super voluminous shiny hair, a super low-cut and super sheer dress and of course super sexy high heel shoes. The silvery, long-sleeve Zuhair Murad dress slivered down my slim but curvy body like they painted it on me.

"I can't believe this is me," I said, in awe of myself as I stared into the full-length mirror.

"Damn, I never thought a woman could leave me speechless. Amazing is the only word I can think of right now."

"And that word describes precisely how I'm feeling."

"You surely look it."

Before I had time to drool over myself any longer I was being rushed to the set, as they were tight on time. When I arrived on the scene Skee Patron didn't even try to conceal how pleased he was with my appearance.

"Where in the fuck did you find her?" he stood and asked coming towards me. "You are fuckin' gorgeous. Where have you been...what other videos have you done? I can't believe I've never seen you before."

"This is actually my first video."

"Yes, she's an actress," Kennedy came out of nowhere and said. "She normally doesn't do videos but you are Skee Patron so we made an exception."

"And you are..."

"Oh, I'm Kennedy, her publicist and this is Blair."

"Blair, I'm honored." Skee extended his hand and I shook it. He didn't seem to want to let it go. I could feel Kirk eyeing us but when I turned towards him he gave me a reassuring smile that let me know he was good.

"Thanks for having me. I'm a fan of your music."

"Then will you be my special guest for my show at Madison Square Garden in a couple weeks? I'll make sure everything is straight for you."

"I..."

"Of course she will," Kennedy said, cutting me off.

"Listen, I have a boyfriend and I don't think he would approve of me attending this concert as your special guest."

"I appreciate your honesty and your loyalty to your man. He's a lucky guy. I tell you what he can come too. Both of you can be my special guest."

"Really?"

"Yes. I'll have my people reach out to your publicist and set everything up for you. Now let's go do this video. I can't wait for the world to see you 'cause you're fuckin' stunning."

Skee Patron had me in awe when he walked off. I wasn't expecting him to respond that way and it threw me off. Although I was watching Skee I could see Kennedy staring at me from the corner of my eye. "Listen, before you give me the riot act..."

"No, no, no, I actually think you handled that very well. My only question to you is who will you be bringing, Michael or Kirk?" Kennedy smirked before walking off.

"That's a wrap!" The video director shouted as everybody on set clapped their hands and pumped their fist. I had a feeling of excitement and exhaustion all at the same time. When I realized what time it was it made perfect sense. It was three o'clock in the morning. We had literally been going nonstop. I changed outfits three times and we kept shooting the same scenes quadruple times. It was completely draining but I loved every minute of it.

"You shined like a star out there."

"Kirk, you're so sweet. I can't believe you stayed here all this time."

"Yo, I told you I take my job seriously. I wasn't going to be done until you're done."

"Thank you," I said and kissed Kirk on the cheek. I'll be right back. I'ma go get out these clothes and then we can go."

"Take your time. I'm not going anywhere."

I felt like I was walking on clouds as I made my way to my dressing room. This was my first real gig and it was with Skee Patron, how lucky could I be.

When I reached my dressing room the first thing I did was check my phone. I had called Michael earlier during a brief break but he didn't answer so I left him a voicemail message. But when I looked at my phone he didn't call or leave a text message. I didn't know if I should be relieved that he wasn't pissed that I was out so late or if I should be disappointed that he didn't seem to care.

"Blair, I'm so proud of you!" The familiar voice shook me out of my thought about Michael. I turned around and saw Kennedy standing in the doorway.

"Thank you! So you think I did a good job?"

"No, you did a great job! Much better than I expected, which makes me, feel wonderful. Now here, fill out this form with your information so they can send you a check."

"I'm getting paid for this?"

"Hell yeah! You're a much sought after actress...at least that's what they think." We both laughed. "But soon you will be. This is just the beginning, Blair."

"Wow, last week I felt my life had no direction and today I have a publicist and I was the lead in a Skee Patron video. I can't believe this is happening for me."

"Well it is."

"Thank you so much, Kennedy."

"You welcome but Diamond is the true angel. Because of her we're both winning right now."

"You're right about that. But ever since we were little girls Diamond has been a gem. She's been through so much but she always thinks about everyone else first. I hope things work out between her and Cameron because she deserves some happiness."

"I hope so too. The three of us have to get together for drinks and celebrate the new direction our lives are going in."

"I agree. Lets make it happen!"

"Will do. And I'll be calling you tomorrow. Now that you've done this video, I'm going to start making some calls and get things lined up. I'm also going to solicit some of the photos that you and Skee took on set to the blogs. They love stuff like this."

"Work your magic because you definitely seem to know what you're doing. Oh, and before you go here's the information you needed. I haven't received a paycheck in so long I'm feeling like a new woman."

"Well, if I work this project the way I intend to, there will be plenty more of these coming in."

"I hope you're right."

"Trust me I am. Get a good night sleep and I won't be calling you early in the morning because hell, by the time you get home the sun might be coming up." Kennedy laughed and quickly disappeared.

By the time I dressed and made my exit Kirk was patiently waiting for me. I couldn't help but feel slightly guilty for thinking so negatively of him just because he was an NBA player. On the other hand Michael would've never sat and waited for me fifteen minutes let alone hours.

"Hey, Superstar. You ready."

"Shut up. You're the superstar."

"In my eyes you're the superstar and soon everybody else will know it too."

"Kirk, thank you."

"For what?"

"For making me feel good about myself."

"If all I have to do is tell the truth then I'll always make you feel good. Now lets go 'cause I know you tired and I damn sure am," Kirk smiled putting his arm around my shoulder. I didn't even feel the need to move his arm away because it felt natural.

"We're here."

"Already, gosh that was quick."

"Yeah, you were quiet during the entire ride I thought you might've fallen asleep."

"No, I was daydreaming. Can you daydream at night?" I couldn't help but giggle at the question.

"You're silly but I don't think there's a specific time of day set aside for daydreaming. I think all you have to do is be awake. Of course I could be wrong. So what were you daydreaming about?"

"Just the direction I want my life to go in. For the first time I feel like I have a real chance at accomplishing something, you know being somebody."

"Blair, you are somebody."

"I mean somebody I can be proud of."

"Why aren't you proud of yourself now?"

"I'm not in school, I don't work, and all I do is depend on a man who makes me feel like I'll never be good enough. Gosh, you must think I'm so pathetic. I can't believe I'm telling you all this."

"I don't think you're pathetic but I do think you're way too hard on yourself. Today was great for you; don't let it end with negative thoughts. Go upstairs and get some rest."

"You're right. Are you going to call me later on?"

"I would love to but I don't have your number."

"Aha ha ha...that's funny and you're right. Get your phone out so I can give it to you."

"Are you sure you want to do that because once I get those digits I'ma be blowing you up."

"Please do." After I gave Kirk my number I stared at him for a few seconds before giving him a kiss. I couldn't help myself. He had these beautiful perfect white teeth with enticing lips. I just wanted to feel them and see if they were as soft as they looked.

"Wow, that was unexpected but nice."

"Sorry, I know I shouldn't have done that."

"No need to apologize. If you like you can do it again and make it longer this time."

"You're such a mess, Kirk. I'm getting out this car before I actually do take you up on your offer. Goodnight."

"Goodnight."

When I got out of Kirk's car and headed towards my apartment building all I could think about was how awesome my entire day had been. If I weren't so exhausted I would never want it to end. But hopefully from this moment forward my life would be filled with many more days just like this.

Diamond

I was sitting on the steps in front of my mother's brownstone watching Destiny ride up and down the street laughing and smiling on her tricycle. It was moments like this, seeing my daughter so happy, that erased the frustrations that came with the line of work I was in.

I was still racking my brain trying to figure out who robbed me and worse did Rico have anything to do with it. I didn't want to believe he did but I knew it was a good possibility. I already hated seeing his face when he came to pick up Destiny but now it was becoming almost unbearable. I had a knot in my stomach right now as I waited for him to pull up to get our daughter for her weekend stay with him. I knew my mind would not be at ease until I finally got some answers to all my questions. But how I would make that happen was the million-dollar question.

"Daddy's here." I heard Destiny's sweet little voice say as she pointed towards Rico's car when he pulled up. He and one of his boys got out and I didn't understand why he always had to bring one of his knucklehead friends with him every time he came over. It was bad enough I had to see him but I shouldn't have to be bothered with anybody else. I realized it was the same annoying guy he came with a few weeks ago. All I could do was roll my eyes.

"I'ma go get Destiny's bag. I'll be right back." I rushed in to get Destiny's stuff so I could get rid of Rico and his boy as quick as possible. When I went back outside Rico and his friend were each holding Destiny's arm swinging her and she was giggling super hard. Because she was having so much fun, at first I wasn't going to say anything but I changed my mind.

"Higher, higher," Destiny kept saying.

"You all need to be careful. I don't want you to dislocate her arm."

"Ain't nobody gon' dislocate her arm. She's having fun...chill."

Dear God I don't feel like arguing with this fool. I know I might be overreacting but please don't let them mess my baby's arms up I thought to myself as I walked up on them.

"Here's her bag." I placed the bag down before going over to interrupt the swinging because the higher they were going the more it was working my nerves. "Come give mommy a kiss goodbye," I said, standing right in front of Destiny so I could grab her as she was coming down. I kissed her on her cheeks and tickled under her arms so she could keep laughing and not feel as if I stopped her fun.

"A'ight, it's time for us to go," Rico said reaching out to get Destiny from me. "Parish, get that bag for me."

"Yo I don't see it, where is it?"

"Behind you," I told him.

"Damn, that shit was right behind me and I didn't even see it."

"What's your name again?"

"Parish, why?"

"You just seem familiar to me."

"I came over to your apartment a few weeks ago with Rico. That's probably where you remember me from."

"Yeah, that's what it is," I said before turning my attention back to my daughter. Destiny, give mommy one more kiss before you go. I'll see you Sunday but I'll call you tomorrow. Have fun."

I kissed Destiny one more time before standing on the sidewalk watching them leave. As much as I couldn't stand Rico, Destiny adored her dad and she loved her weekend visits. Although Rico's mother was the main one taking care of her during her visitations she loved her grandmother too and her cousins. But none of that would matter if Rico had anything to do with the robbery.

After they were gone I went in the house

to make a phone call. I had a gut feeling about something and I had to verify if I was right about it. If I was, things were about to get very interesting so I couldn't dial the number fast enough.

"Yo, what's good?" a voice I was happy to hear said when he answered the phone.

"I have a job for you."

"You know I always like to hear those words. What you got for me?"

"I need you to get all the information you can on a guy named Parish."

"Do you have a last name?"

"Nope but I can tell you where to start looking so you can ask around and get all the information you need."

"You know how I get down, that's all you got to tell me."

"He's with my ex Rico a lot. In fact they are together now. You know where Rico stays so make it happen."

"Say no more I'm on it. I'll have something for you in the next couple days. Is there anything in particular you want me looking out for?"

"Yes. Find out if in the last couple of weeks he seems to have come into a windfall of money. And track his every move. I wanna know what time that nigga shit."

As I browsed the endless aisles of designer clothes at Bergdorf Goodman in search of an outfit for Skee Patron's album release party my mind was somewhere else. I kept on picking up bullshit that I would never wear because I couldn't seem to focus. But the party was tonight and I was about to be assed out if I couldn't get it together. But I couldn't get the sound of Parish voice out of my head. It sounded so familiar. I couldn't help but think he was the one that robbed me. But wasn't a hundred percent sure and before I made a move I had to make sure I was right. The more I thought about it though it did make sense. He had come over to my apartment earlier that day when Rico picked up Destiny and that night I was robbed. My gut was telling me it wasn't a coincidence. If my theory was correct did that mean Rico was in on it. As I pondered all of this I couldn't help but shake my head.

"Shit, that's my phone," I said out loud, once I realized I was so stuck in my thoughts I almost missed the call. "Hey!"

"What's up, what you doing?"

"Shopping, trying to find something to wear tonight."

"Where you going tonight?"

"The album release party...you forgot about it?"

"Damn, that's right. I forgot about that party. I

won't be able to go."

"Why?"

"I have to do something with the team."

"Wow, I was looking forward to seeing you but I guess I understand."

"Girl, I'm just fuckin' wit' you, of course I didn't forget."

"Cameron, you play too much!"

"I know but I can't help myself."

"Whatever."

"So what time should I pick you up?"

"I can meet you in the city because my mom lives in Queens."

"I can come to Queens."

"Are you sure?"

"Of course. What I look like not coming to pick up my girlfriend."

"Did you just call me your girlfriend?"

"Yeah, I did. It just came out. I guess that means you my girl."

"So you don't mind having a girlfriend you've never even had sex with before?"

"We definitely need to work on that but it's different with you, it just feels right."

"I couldn't agree more."

"Not to switch subjects but what's up with your apartment hunting. Marci said she left you several messages but you still haven't returned her call."

"Yeah, I think I'm going to stay with my mom for a little while. Take my time and get myself together before I look for a place."

"I see."

"Tell her I'm sorry I never got back to her."

"I will. So what time should I pick you up?"

"It actually starts pretty early. So 7 is good."

"Cool, I'll see you then."

When I hung up with Cameron I let out a deep sigh. That was the bad thing about lying, once you started it was like you couldn't stop. Now I had one more thing on my mind to add to my frustrations but before I could start feeling sorry for myself this flawless dress was staring me in my face. I practically leaped across the floor to grab it. Once I got it in my hand, all the bullshit that had been cluttering my mind instantly vanished. The only thing I cared about was the low cut, metallic patchwork Balmain mini dress I was holding in my hand. It was beyond gorgeous and I already had the perfect five-inch nude heels to match. In that instant I realized life wasn't so bad after all.

By the time I got home I literally had an hour to get ready. During my commute home I made up my mind that I wouldn't be living in Brooklyn or Queens I would be taking my ass to the City. All that travel time just didn't work for a bitch like me who was horrible with time and always running late. I took a quick shower and spent the remainder of my time on hair and makeup. I was excited about going to the party tonight and more so going with Cameron. I felt this was like our coming out moment. Yeah we had been on plenty of dates together but tonight would be our first industry event as a couple, so I had to make sure my whole look was pure perfection.

"Oh shit, he's here," I shrieked, when I heard the doorbell ringing. Right when I was about to yell out for my mother to let Cameron in I remembered she still hadn't gotten back from dinner and a movie with her own damn boyfriend. I hated to feel rushed but luckily I was basically done getting ready. I just preferred to have some extra time so I could thoroughly scrutinize myself before walking out the door. Instead I had to do a quick look over and keep my fingers crossed that everything was right and tight. I rushed downstairs and took a deep breath before opening the door with a welcoming smile on my face.

"Damn!" Cameron belted, as his eyes zigzagged up and down my body. "My fault, I didn't mean to be so loud. I hope your mother didn't hear me."

"No worries, she's out," I grinned. "So I guess you approve of my dress?"

"Approve," he paused for a second as if he couldn't believe I was even asking the question. "I more than approve. I don't think I'll be able to keep my hands off of you tonight."

"I don't want you to...let's go." Cameron and I held hands as we walked to his car. He opened the passenger door for me like the perfect gentleman he always is. "Thank you, I beamed, feeling like this night couldn't get any better although it was just getting started.

"You really do look beautiful tonight," Cameron said, as he merged onto I-278 W/Brooklyn Queens Expressway.

"You make me feel beautiful."

"I do...how?"

"Little things you say and how you treat me."

"I only treat you the way you deserve to be treated," Cameron said, reaching over to take my hand. I sat back and closed my eyes wishing this night would never end. "You don't mind if I make that stop do you?"

"Of course not. We're together, that's all that matters. You can go wherever you like."

If only for tonight I was going to throw all the negative thoughts out the window. No stressing about Rico and Parish or my living situation. In my head I was screaming fuck the bullshit and embrace the moment. If Cameron weren't in the car with me I would've yelled it out loud.

"What's so funny?" Cameron asked when I laughed out loud over what I was just thinking about.

"Nothing just remembering something

Destiny did the other day," I lied, not wanting to share my personal thoughts.

"I can't wait to meet your daughter."

"Really?"

"Yeah, why do you sound like you're surprised?"

"I don't know. I just didn't think you were into kids like that."

"Anybody that's important to you I'm interested in. I guess I feel like when you're ready for me to meet your daughter then I must be important in your life."

"Cameron you are. Please don't take it that way. I always promised myself that I wouldn't have different men in and out of Destiny's life."

"I figured that and that's why I know if you let me meet her then you must think we have something special although I already know we do."

"I believe that too and I apologize if I made you think otherwise."

"It's okay, I'm not pressuring you. When you're ready you'll let me know. I just wanted you to understand that if you're holding back because of me, don't because I am ready."

"I can't believe how amazing you are."

"I feel the same way about you...we're here, come on." I looked out the window and Cameron had pulled in front of a luxury high rise on Central Park West.

"How many cribs do you have, I mean you are

only one person," I commented. I had already been to one condo Cameron had on the Upper East Side but I guess when you making serious bankroll that's the type of shit you do. "This place is beautiful," I said when we walked through the marble entry way towards the elevator.

"Yeah, I said the same thing myself the first time I came through the doors."

"It must be nice to be able to afford the best in life."

"Honestly, the best thing about having money is being able to look out for your people and make sure they are straight. Knowing you're able to do that is the best feeling in the world."

"I can only imagine."

When Cameron opened the door my mouth dropped. The marble theme carried over into the entrance of the apartment with wide plank hardwood floors throughout. I mean this fucking place had it all, recessed lighting, high-grade base molding and crown molding. When we entered the kitchen there was a double stainless steel sink, wolf appliances, granite counter tops and even a walk-in pantry. There were his and her custom bathrooms with steam showers. To top everything off there was a private octagonal shaped balcony that went from the master bedroom all the way to the living room. What appeared to be 12-and-a-half-foot ceilings made the already humongous place look even more open and spacious.

"Do you love it as much as I do?"

"Is that a trick question or a joke! This place is beyond beautiful."

"Not only is it beautiful but the amenities are out of this world. I'm talking concierge, bellman, valet parking, indoor pool, fitness center, spa and the best thing is it has complete security and key control. You can't get no safer than that."

"I see there's no furniture. Did you just get this place?"

"Yep, I got the keys yesterday."

"Wow, I can't wait to see how it looks after the furniture is moved in and it's decorated."

"I can't wait to see it either. So when are you going to get started."

"When am I gonna get started," I said with an almost choked voice.

"Yep. I got this place for you and Destiny." This time I really did choke. "Are you okay?" Cameron ran towards me because for a second I truly believe I almost stopped breathing.

"I'm fine. But Cameron you really shouldn't joke with me like that. You literally almost gave me a heart attack."

"Diamond, I would tell you to come sit down but there ain't no chairs and I don't want you sitting on the floor because you might mess up your dress so lean on me if you need support after I say this. I got this apartment for you. It's not a joke. I felt some kinda way that you were living in an apartment that you didn't feel safe in then you had to stay with your mom because you couldn't afford to get a nice place on your own. What kind of man would I be if I'm calling you my woman but I can't look out for you?"

"Cameron, I don't deserve this from you. I can't accept it. I'm almost too stunned to believe this is even true."

"It is true and please accept it. I told Marci I wanted her to find the perfect spot for you and Destiny and when she showed me this place it had your name written all over it."

"I can't...I just can't," I kept saying, shaking my head.

"I already signed a one year lease, you have to take it."

"Are you serious?"

"Yes. I want you to stay here. I figured within a year we'll both know how far we want things to go in this relationship."

"I hope it doesn't but I always try to be realistic. What if we fall out, I can't afford to pay the rent on this place."

"I knew you would be concerned about that so I already paid the rent up for a year."

"What." My voice went low and I could feel tears welling up in my eyes.

"Babe, don't you dare cry," Cameron said,

gently rubbing the side of my face.

"I don't know what I did to deserve you. All I can think is that somebody is praying awfully hard for me."

"You are too much."

"No you are. No matter what happens between us I'll never forget what you did for me and my daughter."

"Does that mean you'll take the place?"

"Hell yeah!" I burst out laughing. Then Cameron picked me up and swung me around before we embraced in a long kiss. It was like we brought out the kid in each other. Our bond was real and I wanted it to last forever.

Kennedy

"Rise and shine, Blair! You have a busy, busy next couple of days so I hope your mind is right and your energy is up."

"I'm good. I know the concert is tonight and then tomorrow is the party but what else is going on?"

"Lionsgate is having a luncheon today for the cast of their new movie with Tyler Blake. We're doing all the PR for the movie so of course I can get you into the luncheon."

"Are you serious?"

"Yes. I know it's late notice but I told you, you always have to be ready."

"And I am. Tell me the time and I'll be there."

"Great! That's what I like to hear. It's in the private dining room at the Four Seasons Hotel. A ton of bigwigs will be in attendance and a lot of press so you need to look picture perfect. So I've already called my girl Eileen to come over to your place at eleven o'clock to do your hair and makeup. The event starts at two. I want you to wear a dress. Something that showcases your figure but understated, you know very classy. Like you're not trying to showoff but it's not your fault you're drop dead gorgeous. You feel me...do you have a dress like that?"

"I totally get it. I think I have the perfect dress."

"Are you sure because if not I'll send Tammy out to get you something."

"I'm positive."

"I'll take your word since you're pretty much on point every time I see you. But I need you to bring your super A game today. This is truly a make it moment. I have big plans for you so we have to work this right."

"I won't let you down, Kennedy. Trust me I don't want to ruin this. You've done so much for me already. Way more than I've ever imagined. I want us to go all the way."

"Keep following my lead and we will. I'll be in touch these next couple of hours and I'll see you soon."

"Cool."

"Kennedy, the queen bee told me to have you come to her office," Tammy told me as soon as I hung up with Blair.

"What does she want," I mumbled rolling my eyes.

"Not sure, but no need to rush."

"Why do you say that? You know how Darcy hates waiting on anybody."

"She won't notice. Some ridiculously handsome guy in an expensive suit is in there keeping her company."

"Really?"

"Yep."

"Do I know him?"

"I don't know. His face does look somewhat familiar but it could be that I saw him at some of the events we've done. Not sure, but I do know I've never seen Darcy act so sweet and flirty around a guy before. I almost forgot she's an ice queen."

"Yeah, it would be interesting to meet the guy who can bring that out of her. But anyway, while I'm talking to our boss," I uttered sarcastically, "confirm the press for Skee Patron's album release party tomorrow."

"So is that all we're covering for his party?"

"Yeah, his label is doing the actual event all we're handling is the press and guest list."

"Sweet. That party is going to rock. Goodness, I hope I get to meet Skee."

"I take it you're a fan."

"Of course, who isn't a fan!"

"I'm not big on his music but he's winning right now so good for him. But tomorrow night, remember we are working so no groupie antics."

"I got you. I promise to be on my best behavior."

"I counting on it," I said, winking my eye before

I turned to go to Darcy's office. As soon as I came out the door I bumped straight into a solid six-foot with some inches man. "I'm so sorry, excuse me."

"In the future when you're walking, don't look down at the floor, look up. It will make it much easier for you to avoid this type of misstep."

"Is there a problem?" Darcy questioned, stepping out of her office."

"Again, I apologize."

"No, there isn't a problem. It's been dealt with," he replied in a self-important tone. While giving him a smug side-eye on the low it quickly hit me that I remembered this arrogant fuck. He was the prick Darcy was tonguing down when she had me come into work on a Saturday morning. He walked past me like I was beneath him because I was dressed down on some bum shit. It was amazing to me that Darcy was all love struck over a dude that had a worse attitude than her. But maybe that's what she liked. He had to be the ultimate challenge for her because he probably treated her like shit.

"Is he a new client, Darcy?" I asked, playing dumb like I didn't know what was up.

"No, he's actually my man." After Darcy said it, her face lit up like fireworks. I was stunned she even admitted that shit.

"This is a first. I've never heard you acknowledge having a man."

"That's because no man has ever deserved it

until now. But enough about my personal life, we're in the workplace so lets stick to business."

"Whatever you say, you're the boss."

"Exactly, and because I'm the boss I have to personally take a trip to LA and meet with a potential big money client."

"I'm sure you'll lock that deal down."

"I'm sure I will too but I need for you to hold things down for me until I get back."

"How long will you be gone?"

"A week."

"Wow, this must be a really important client to keep you away from the office for a week."

"It is. Plus I'm going to make the most of the trip and meet with some other clients too. But I need you to stay on top of everything while I'm gone, Kennedy."

"Have I ever let you down?"

"No, and I don't want you to start now. I will be here for Skee Patron's party tomorrow night but then I'm flying out first thing in the morning. Of course we'll be in constant contact throughout my trip but I expect for you to make sure everything runs smoothly during my absence."

"Darcy, don't you worry. I plan to run this business like it's my very own. So you go to LA and get that money." I gave Darcy a reassuring smile and I wanted to do cartwheels exiting her office. A week of not having to see Darcy's face was a dream come true and more importantly with her not hovering over me it would give me so much time to work Blair's project. This was fantastic news.

I was looking at my watch as I waited in the lobby of the Four Seasons Hotel for Blair. It was 1:55pm and I was keeping my fingers crossed she would be on time. I wanted to get her posted up in the luncheon and knock out a few photo opps before Darcy got there. Because if Darcy caught me working the room on Blair's behalf she would grill me like she was the feds.

"Omigoodness! Blair, I can't believe you're early," I gasped, as I saw her coming towards me.

"Only a few minutes."

"I don't know when you're going to listen to me when I tell you that every second counts. You're slowly becoming my favorite client, although technically you're my only client. But enough about that, come with me and by the way you look amazing."

"So this works for you?"

"Yes, I'm loving this cut and the aqua color is going to show beautiful on photos. And color-block peeptoes sets the dress off perfectly. Then the hair and makeup, you are truly looking like a star. Come, come, come, we have to work this room quick," I said, taking Blair's hand leading her into the limelight.

"So happy you approve."

The moment we entered the private dining room I began introducing Blair to movie executives and having her take pictures with A and B list stars in attendance. The great thing about these type of intimate private events was that mostly everybody arrived early or right on time because they knew it didn't last that long so they wanted to do as much politicking as they possibly could.

"Marcus, hi, it's so good to see you."

"Kennedy, how are you? It's been a long time."

"I know. You're so busy making moves in Hollywood you have no time for us little people," I joked.

"Please, I see you're still making moves. Always in the right places."

"I'm trying and as a matter of fact I want you to meet a new client of mine."

"I had no idea you started your own PR Company. But between us, I always thought you had way too much potential to just be under Darcy."

"I'm actually still working for Darcy but I'm slowly but surly branching out on my own and Blair is my first client. Blair, "I called out, motioning for her to come over. There was some young up and coming director all up in her face, which was good but Marcus was so much better.

"That's your new client?"

"Yep."

"I see why she's your first client. She is a real beauty."

"And you know what else, she has real talent and I'm not just saying that because I rep her. Marcus you need to give this girl a chance."

"You mean like an audition?"

"Yes, she's an actress, not simply a pretty face."

"I apologize that it took me so long to get over here but that director had so much to say but it was all good stuff."

"No problem. I was calling you over here because I wanted you to meet Marcus Powell. He is the top guy over at Lionsgate. He actually played a major role in getting the Tyler Perry deal done over there."

"It's a pleasure to meet you, Mr. Powell."

"The pleasure is all mine but please call me Marcus."

"And I'm Blair."

"I know. Kennedy can't stop singing your praises."

"Well thank you, Kennedy."

"I'm only speaking the truth."

"So how long have you been acting, Blair?" Marcus asked, quickly warming up to Blair. From the corner of my eye I noticed Darcy coming our way.

"Excuse me for a moment. I'll be back but while I'm gone you all get acquainted," I smiled before hurrying off towards Darcy. "Darcy, you made it," I casually greeted her, hoping she didn't catch I was trying to stop her in her tracks.

"Yes, I did. The event seems to be going very nicely. The turnout is even better than I expected. The combination of high ranking executives and movie stars is balanced perfectly."

"I was thinking the exact same thing."

"Who is that young woman Marcus Powell is talking to?"

"I think some new actress on the scene."

"She must have some pretty good connects to get into a luncheon like this."

"I have no idea."

"I wonder if she has a rep. Let me go introduce myself."

"Darcy, Idris Elba is waving for you to come over. You can go talk to that girl later, he's *way* more important."

"Oh, Idris is here...yeah she can wait," Darcy said to my relief. No, Idris didn't wave for Darcy to come over but her ego was so colossal she would believe it and that's all that mattered. As I followed behind her all I could think to myself was she couldn't get on that flight to LA soon enough.

Blair

I was still smiling when I got back to my apartment after the luncheon. I couldn't believe all the incredible people I met and the amount of pictures that were taken of me. Kennedy was going out her way to see me succeed and it was paying off big time. But one thing she was right about is that I was constantly on the move. I hadn't had a moment of sleeping late and being on chill mode since she took on my project. I had to catch a moment of rest anytime I could get it and that's what I planned on doing. I was about to take off my clothes so I could get a couple hours of sleep before getting ready for Skee's concert tonight. But before I could even take my shoes off and relax I could hear the front door opening.

"Michael, I'm surprised to see you. I thought you said you weren't coming over until it was time to go to the concert."

"There has been a change of plans."

"Meaning?"

"I can't make it the concert tonight."

"Why not?"

"An important meeting had to be rescheduled for later on tonight and I know it's going to run late."

"You can't reschedule it for tomorrow morning instead."

"Did you not hear me use the word important?"

"It seems everything but me is important to you."

"Really, Blair. Are you about to bore me with one of your tantrums? I came here to see you and let you know I couldn't make it tonight not to listen to you complain."

"Wanting to spend time with my boyfriend is complaining? I haven't even had the chance to talk to you and let you know all the great things that have been going on in my life lately."

"I'm sure it's nothing that I would be interested in."

"You're so cold."

"I'm not cold I'm honest. What could possibly be the highlight of your day...getting your hair colored? Buying a new pair of shoes, bag and dress. Like I said nothing interesting."

"You really don't believe in me at all. I'll never be good enough for you."

"We've already established that so why are you even bringing it up and making it a part of our discussion."

"Michael, why…"

"Damn," he said reading a text message. "I have to go. I'll call you later."

"Can't that wait? We're not finished talking."

"We are finished for now. I have to go. I'll call you later." Without saying another word Michael simply left me standing in the middle of the living room feeling worthless. The high I was just on from being at the luncheon, mingling with the Hollywood elite had been yanked from me. With a slow stride I went in my bedroom full of gloom. I hated that such a depressing feeling had come over me. I wanted to close my eyes and just sleep but then I heard my phone ringing. My first reaction was that Michael realized how cruel he had been and was calling to apologize, of course that was wishful thinking.

"Hey, Kennedy, what's up?"

"I just got off the phone with Skee's people and I was calling to give you the time the limo would be picking you all up and where to go when you get to Madison Square Garden."

"I'm not gonna be able to make it."

"Excuse me…what do you mean you're not going to be able to make it?"

"Michael just left and he can't come tonight."

"And what difference does that make?"

"He was the one that was supposed to go with me."

"I seriously doubt if Skee cares that your

boyfriend can't attend the concert with you."

"I don't want to go by myself."

"Call Diamond. I'm sure she would love to go."

"No, that's okay. I really don't feel like going anymore."

"Blair, please don't make me stop my work and drag you to that concert. I have too much shit to get done to drop everything and hold your hand."

"I'm not asking you to hold my hand. Can't I have a moment to myself because my boyfriend made me feel like shit and I don't want to be bothered with anybody?"

"Nope, you don't have that luxury when you're a new talent trying to build a career."

"This is a fuckin' concert it isn't work!"

"That's where you're wrong. Sweetie, in this business you're always on the clock working. This isn't just a concert. You're the leading lady in Skee Patron's upcoming video. That exposure is going to lead to more work. When you go to that concert tonight that's a photo opp I can use to get more press for you. When you're in the VIP area, tastemakers will see your face and you'll network. Again, this is all work. So you're going to stop feeling sorry for yourself, get up off your ass and go to that concert. I don't give a damn if a bum off the street is your date, you're going, are we clear?"

"Yes, we're clear."

"Good. The limo will be there at seven-thirty. I

will text you all the other information."

"Fine."

"And, Blair."

"Yes."

"I expect you to be a professional tonight. Leave the sour face at home. Every time you walk out that door, you are representing a star and you have to conduct yourself as such. If you don't look and act the part then you'll never get the part. Understood?"

"Understood."

"Wonderful. I'll be in touch with you later on." When I hung up with Kennedy I immediately called Diamond."

"Hey girl, what is going on?"

"I'm so glad you answered the phone."

"Of course. I've wanted to talk to you. We've been playing phone tag for the last week or so."

"I know things have been so crazy."

"Kennedy told me. She's really been busting her ass for you but she said you're worth it because you've been doing everything she's told you to do and you guys are having great success."

"Yeah, that's true. But ummm..."I tried to hold back my tears but I couldn't stop the sniffling.

"Blair, what's wrong...are you okay?"

"No I'm not."

"What happened?"

"Take a guess?"

"Ahhh shit, it has to be that asshole Michael.

Only he can make you cry a river."

"Diamond, he is so mean. It's like every time I start feeling good about myself he totally shatters it." My voice was quivering and I was becoming way more emotional than I had intended.

"I hate that you let him do this to you. Enough is enough, Blair. If you don't let Michael go, he's going to emotionally destroy you."

"I can't help but believe deep down inside he does love me."

"Girl, that ain't love it's called mental abuse. He uses that to control you."

"Listen, Kennedy made it very clear that I have to attend this Skee Patron concert tonight. Would you please go with me?"

"Fuck I would love to but I promised my mother I would take her to Jersey to visit her best friend who just got out of the hospital. I'm so sorry. Why don't you call Kirk?"

"I don't know. I don't want him to get the wrong idea."

"What idea is that...that you're available? Please, Blair that's exactly what he needs to believe and it needs to be true."

"It's much more complicated than that."

"Look, my mother is calling for me to come on so I have to go. But call Kirk and go to the concert with him. Ever since we were little girls you've been so sensitive and I would always try to protect you but Blair I need you to start protecting yourself."

"I know and you're right."

"I'll see you tomorrow night at the party but we'll talk before then. Now call Kirk!" Diamond yelled out before hanging up.

All I wanted to do was crawl into bed and cry my heart out but instead of taking the easy way out I dialed Kirk's number. "Is this who I think it is?" Kirk answered in his typical charming voice.

"How are you? Did I catch you at a bad time?"

"No. But it seems every time I try to call you it must be at a bad time because you never answer."

"Sorry about that but things have been so hectic for me since the video shoot. Kennedy keeps me extremely busy."

"That means she's on her job which is how it's supposed to be."

"I can't complain. Kennedy is definitely making it happen. Speaking of making things happen. I know it's last minute and I totally understand if you have other plans but I wondering if you would attend Skee Patron's concert with me tonight?"

"Mos Def."

"Really...wow....thanks." For some reason I didn't think Kirk would be available on such short notice but it was amazing how he always made time for me when I did need him unlike Michael.

"Thank you for inviting me although I'm sure I wasn't your first choice. But that's okay, I'll take a date with you anyway I can get it. What time do you want me to pick you up?'

"Actually, Skee arranged for a limo to come get us. We're his special invited guests. Is that cool with you?"

"You mean you're his special invited guest but I'm cool with that. We're going to have a good time and that's all that matters."

"You're right." To my amazement I found myself smiling. I would've never guessed that speaking with Kirk would lift my spirit. I was so happy I took Diamond's advice and made the call. "So can you be here around seven-fifteen?"

"Sure can. I'll see you then."

"Yeah, see you then. Bye, Kirk."

After hanging up with Kirk I was no longer in the mood to take an afternoon nap. Instead I turned on some music and blasted it really loud. I found myself dancing around my apartment to Rhianna's new feel good song and that high that had been yanked from me was now back.

Diamond

"Cameron, let us get a shot of you," several photographers were screaming out when we arrived at the party. At first Cameron was going to skip the red carpet but the press was making it difficult.

"Would you mind walking the red carpet with me and taking some pictures?"

"You don't have to have me in the pics. You go 'head."

"I want you in them with me if you don't mind."

"You're gonna make me blush."

"That's cool but do it after they snap these pics," we both laughed. When we hit the carpet the flashbulbs instantly started blinding me.

"Who is the young lady with you? What's her name? Is she your girlfriend?" The questions were rolling off all the photographers tongue quicker than Cameron could answer them.

"Yes, she's my girlfriend and her name is Diamond." Once Cameron said that it was on and poppin'. They came at me like vultures.

"Diamond, turn this way. No turn this way. What do you do for a living? How did you and Cameron meet?" They were relentless with the questions and the only reason I got through it was because Cameron was by my side.

"How do you deal with this shit?" I asked once we were done and in the building.

"You get used to it."

"I don't think I could ever get used to all that attention."

"I said the same thing when I first got in the league. But dealing with the press, it's part of the business which means it's part of my job. And how can I complain with all the money I make. Yes, it's a curse but it's also a major blessing. So you have to take the good with the bad."

"When you explain it like that you're right."

"I don't want this craziness to scare you off but if you're gonna be by my side, you have to get used to this. This is my life."

"It's gonna take much more than this to scare me away from you."

"That's what I wanted to hear," Cameron said, leaning down to give me a kiss.

When we got in the party the first person we ran into was Blair who was looking every bit the superstar in a palilette-embellished white strapless dress with sparkly Jimmy Choos and a crimson lip.

"Girl, I swear I was gonna get those shoes but they didn't have my size in stock and I was pissed. Bitch, you look fuckin' amazing!"

"You're so sweet, Diamond, but you look unbelievable tonight. I guess we both were aiming for the best-dressed award."

"Who did you come with?"

"Kirk. He should be back in a minute. He had to go to the bathroom."

"What! First the concert now this party, that's two dates in a row. I'm so proud of you."

"I'm kinda proud of myself. But Kirk makes it so easy. He's so laid back and cool with everything. I never feel stressed or under pressure when I'm with him."

"That's because he's a good guy."

"Speaking of good guys you and Cameron seem awfully tight." I turned around to see what Cameron was doing before I spoke. He was occupied talking to some dude so I felt free to do some sharing with Blair.

"Girl, before we came over here he took me to this freakin' apartment that is too fly for words and guess what?"

"What?"

"He got it for me and Destiny."

"Stop playing!"

"I'm so serious. He wanted us to have our own place and not have to stay with my mom. And just so

I could have a certain level of security, he paid the rent up for a year. Is this dude heaven sent or what?"

"You have truly hit the jackpot, Diamond but if anybody deserves it, it's you. You're always looking out for everybody else, I'm so glad somebody is finally looking out for you."

"But do you know we haven't even had sex yet. I'm starting to think there may be some truth to holding out on the goods might get you the prize."

"So you're going to keep holding out?"

"Hell no! He's proven himself to be worthy. I'm just saying that I believe by making him wait and not fucking his brains out off the jump made him have to take the time to get to know me and develop real feelings beside just sexual ones. You know what I'm saying?"

"I do, that's a good point. When you wait and don't have sex with somebody you do get a chance to see who they really are. When you have sex too soon it blurs your mind from making rational decisions."

"That's my point."

"I sure hope things work out for you and Cameron because I can't lie. The first time the two of you even met there was undeniable chemistry. It was like you all had known each other forever, you just clicked."

"So true. That's my baby...hold on, I have to take this call."

"Sure." I went over to a corner to try and get

some privacy before answering.

"What's good?"

"I have some information for you."

"Already? I thought it would take you much longer?"

"You said it was an emergency so I got right on it. And we got lucky 'cause one of my homeboys be in that neighborhood that Parish lives in a lot. So he know everything the streets talking 'bout."

"So what you find out?"

"That nigga got diarrhea of the mouth. He been tellin' everybody and they mother that will listen that he got this chick for a 100 stacks and he planning on going back for more."

"I knew it was that dirty dick nigga who robbed me!"

"Yo' gut instinct was right. So what you want me to do?"

"You already know how this shit is going down."

"I'm on it then."

"Hold on. Did your guy hear anything about Rico, like was he in on it?"

"From what my partner heard it was a one man operation which consisted of only Parish."

"Cool. Well you know what to do."

"I got you. I'll call you when it's done." I wanted to toss my IPhone across the fuckin' room I was so pissed. I despised the fact that the snake who robbed me, my enemy had been in my space and around my daughter. The only thing that gave me solace was the nigga would be deleted soon. The only other thing that made this bitter pill a little easier to swallow was that Rico wasn't involved. I couldn't stand the nigga but Destiny adores her daddy and I would've hated to delete that nigga too.

"Is everything okay?" I was startled and jumped when I felt Cameron's hand on my shoulder and heard his voice. "I didn't mean to scare you. You ok did something happen?"

"I'm good. My mother has some personal things going on and she was just talking my ear off but I'm fine."

"Is your mother okay?"

"Oh yeah, she's fine. My mother can be extra dramatic sometimes. But everything is good with her. But you know what I would like."

"What, tell me?"

"I would love for us to leave."

"You're not enjoying the party? You're ready to go back home already? I was looking forward to spending some time with you tonight."

"That's what I want too. But instead of sharing you with a crowd I would rather have some alone time with you."

"Really, you want some alone time with me?"

"Yes. So what's it gonna be? Stay here and mingle or go back to your place and get to know each other even better?"

"Babe, you ain't said nothing but a thang...lets go." Cameron took my hand and rushed me outta there so fast I didn't even have time to say goodbye to Blair or even see Kennedy. But they could wait because I was anxious to finally be with my man.

It felt like we had snapped our fingers and went from the party to Cameron's bed, that's how fast we seemed to have gotten there. We couldn't keep our hands off each other. All this sexual tension had built up and we were like two animals clawing at each other. When Cameron unzipped my dress, as he slid it down he kissed every curve on my body until it had fallen to the floor. Then he lifted me up like I was as light as paper and wrapped my legs around his waist. His muscular arms held me up, as my hardened nipples got lost in his moist mouth. He swallowed them like he couldn't get enough.

"Oh Cameron," I moaned as his tongue went back and forth teasing each breast until all I wanted was all of him inside of me. The more I moaned the more he licked and kissed until laying me down on the bed and lifting my ass up while his tongue went from my nipples to my sugar walls. The strokes of his tongue started slow and deliberate touching each part of my clit with precision. As Cameron's tongue went deeper and deeper inside of me, he began working me into a frenzy. My legs were shaking in anticipation of the climax I felt my body about to reach. Then when I thought I couldn't take anymore he stopped.

"You tasted so good."

"Why did you stop?" I asked in a low tone because I was practically out of breath.

"Because my tongue tasted you now my dick wants to feel inside of you." Cameron stood up and took off his shirt, pants and when he stepped out of his boxers my heart dropped for a second. I had seen my fair share of dicks but his shit was seriously intimidating. And clearly Cameron could see the fear in my eyes.

"Baby, I'll be gentle. I'll try my hardest not to hurt you." Now it made sense why this nigga wasn't stressing me for sex, he probably knew I would be ready to run for dear life.

"Cameron, to say you're very well endowed would be an understatement."

"If you don't want to go any further I understand."

"No I want to."

"Are you sure?"

"I'm positive." And as big as Cameron's dick was I did want to continue. His tongue action had me so horny I was willing to take whatever pain he brought my way. I leaned forward and locked lips with Cameron, letting him know I was serious. The fear I felt was the type I welcomed. I positioned myself comfortably on the bed never losing eye contact with him. He took the tip of his dick and gently slid it up and down the center of my wet pussy as the juices dripped on the tip. With each slide he gently maneuvered the thickness of his tool deeper inside of me. My cries of pleasure and pain became louder and louder until all of him was resting peacefully inside of me. My legs had spread so far apart so my insides could welcome all of him.

"Oh, Diamond, you don't know how fuckin' good you feel. I wish my dick could stay inside of you forever."

"Me too," I purred, loving how he filled me up. After a few minutes my walls seemed to become comfortable with having Cameron's dick inside of me and my ass and hips were able to get into it and move to the rhythm of his thrust. "Baby, I love you I found myself saying. I couldn't help myself and I didn't want to.

"Diamond, I love you too." Those were the last words I remembered hearing before losing myself in complete ecstasy.

In the middle of the night I woke up cuddled up under Cameron. I didn't want to move but I had to go to the bathroom so bad. I slid from up under him slowly trying my best not to wake him because he was sleeping so peacefully. I was somewhat sore when I got up but my crazy ass was ready to have that dick right back up in me after I finished going to the bathroom. Before I went though I decided to check my phone. I saw that I missed that dudes call so I took my cell in the bathroom with me so I could hit him back. When I called it rang a few times and then went to voicemail. I tried one more time and it did the same shit. I figured he called to let me know everything was done and I could sleep in peace knowing that snake was a thing of the past, and now he was probably knocked out. So I went to the bathroom, washed my hands and got back in bed with my man so we could have a round two. First I was scared of the dick now I couldn't get enough of it.

Kennedy

It had been four days since Darcy had been gone and I was dreading the fact she would be back in three. I had been so productive with my own shit with her out the way. With the photos I got of Blair from the multiple events she attended over the last few weeks, I was able to service them to all the major blogs and from that it sparked interest from several print magazines. Many of them set up interviews with her and I was working on getting some features. This required a lot of talking on the phone and back and forth with emails. If Darcy had been in the office I would've never been able to get all this done. Right when I was about to follow up with another potential lead my cell started ringing and it was an LA number.

"Fuck, I wonder if this is Darcy calling me from a landline," I said out loud not wanting to hear her voice. "Hello."

"Hey, Kennedy, this is Marcus Powell. Did I

catch you at a bad time."

"No, not at all. How are you?"

"I'm great. It was really good seeing you last week. And I enjoyed talking to Blair. That young lady has a lot of potential."

"I told you. Does that mean you're calling because you have a movie role for her?"

"Not yet but I promise you she is on my mind. And when I believe the right part has come up I will definitely be giving you a call so she can come in for an audition."

"I'm going to hold you to that, Marcus."

"Kennedy, you know I'm a straight shooter. I don't say anything I don't mean."

"You won't get an argument with me about that. So I'm sure a busy man like you didn't call just to tell me that."

"No, I actually have a job proposition for you. You told me you're trying to branch out and you need clients in order to do that."

"I'm listening."

"I've seen you in action I know your work ethic and I believe you won't disappoint me. That's why I want you on this project."

"So what's the project?"

"Lionsgate is having me oversee a new small movie division and I want you to handle the PR."

'That might be a little difficult since you're based in LA."

"We're having a main office that will be located in New York so you're right where you need to be. If you do decide to take the project on you will have to travel to LA on occasion but you'll be handling mostly everything from New York. And it's paying $10,000 a month."

"Nothing like that movie money."

"Yeah, our budgets are a little bit bigger."

"So are you in?"

"Let me think it over. When do you need your answer?"

"As soon as possible but by the end of the week will suffice."

"I will definitely be in touch."

"Kennedy, this is an incredible opportunity. I hope you don't let it slip through your fingers. Hope to hear from you soon. Bye."

"Bye, and Marcus, thanks for thinking of me."

"Always my pleasure.'"

When I hung up with Marcus I looked at my watch and realized I was late for my lunch date with Diamond. I grabbed my purse and headed out because not only did I hate being late I was also starving.

"Diamond, I'm so sorry I'm late!" I said sitting down at the table.

"Girl please, as many times you've had to wait

on me. "

"But you know how anal I am when it comes to being punctual. I got caught up on some business calls and got completely sidetracked."

"I figured you got caught up in work since that's all you do."

"What can I say I'm a workaholic."

"I admire that about you though."

"Trust me, there's nothing to admire about that. So you know I always love spending time with you but when you called you made it sound so urgent that we meet. What's going on? Wait, before you get started let me order something to eat. I haven't had a bite of anything all day and you know how evil I can get when I'm starving."

"Oh I know. That's why I already put your order in for your favorite...the grilled chicken Cobb salad. And of course I got your Bellini."

"Diamond, you are the best. So go 'head, Honey, no more interruptions from me."

"So, I've been thinking and I came up with somewhat of a brilliant idea."

"Do tell because if anybody can come up with a brilliant idea is you."

"As you know I've made a lot of investments that have paid off very well for me financially and I wanted to do something that could help me build a future."

"Something like what?"

"Like starting my own business or maybe partnering up with someone." Diamond was giving me this weird look and I wasn't able to get a read.

"I think starting your own business would be a good look. You just have to make sure you pick something you know a lot about and that you partner with somebody that's also bringing something to the table since you're the one who's coming with the money."

"I totally agree. That's why I was thinking we could partner up together"

"Us, doing what?"

"A public relations company. You've been saying how sick you are of working for Darcy. She's never going to pay you what you deserve so why don't you be your own boss. We could be 50/50 partners."

"Are you serious, Diamond? I had no idea you had an interest in PR."

"I'm a people person and love going out that's a start."

"I suppose but you do know how much work and dedication comes into starting a new company?"

"Of course. Kennedy, you know I always give my all at whatever I do."

"True but this isn't a job you'll be doing on your own you'll have a partner."

"I understand that but I think we would make great partners. I know it won't be easy but I think it's worth trying. You don't agree?"

"I do think we would be good partners but I just don't want to…" my voice trailed off.

"Want to what, say it."

"You're the one that's bringing the money."

"But you're bringing the experience."

"What if that's not enough and I disappoint you?"

"Is that what you're worried about?"

"Yes. I would hate to partner up with you and then I don't meet your expectations."

"Anytime you do a startup you're taking risks but that's part of the business. But I rather take those risks with you than with anybody else."

"I feel the same way. This might actually work. And you know what, I did get a call today about taking on a new project for a small movie studio and they are offering $10,000 a month. I was reluctant about taking it on because I felt it might be too much for me to take on by myself but if I had a partner I would feel more confident about doing so. And I know Tammy my intern would definitely want to join our team."

"So does this mean you're in?"

"Yeah…I think I am. Make that a yes!"

"Kennedy, you will not regret this. We're going to make an awesome team."

"So you're positive this is what you want and you're not going to change your mind?"

"I do want this and I need it."

"What do you mean you need it?"

"I just want to get my life right. Cameron and I are getting serious and I want him to be proud of me."

"Diamond, I've never heard you talk like that before. Anybody would be proud of you. Although you don't have some big time career you're clearly done well for yourself financially by making very smart business investments. So of course Cameron is proud of you."

"I'm just ready to accomplish more and us having this company together will give me a chance to do that."

"Well, I'm excited and I think this is a great new beginning for both of us."

"Yes it is. Now lets eat, drink and be merry."

"Cheers!" We said in unison and clicked our champagne glasses.

Blair

As I rushed to get dressed for some dinner at this industry guys penthouse that Kennedy insisted I attend I realized I couldn't stop thinking about Kirk. For the last couple of weeks we had been spending so much time together but it was more as friends then anything else but I couldn't shake missing him. Instead of going to some dinner and being around a bunch of industry people I didn't know I would've much rather been spending time with Kirk, but like Kennedy kept drilling in my head on a daily basis, work first. So when my phone started ringing there was no doubt in my mind it was her calling.

"Hello, Kennedy."

"Are you almost ready?"

"Yes. I'm putting on my shoes now."

"Good because I'm downstairs in the car waiting for you."

"I'm on my way down." I glanced at my reflection one last time in the mirror and headed downstairs. I was becoming more and more convinced that Kennedy was a man in a woman's body because I had never met a female that was more consumed with work in all my life. She reminded me of Michael in that regard. Kennedy never talked about dating, going on a vacation, shopping, none of that. All she cared about was work and there was no doubt she was excellent at what she did but I didn't think it was healthy for someone so young to eat, drink and sleep work.

When I got outside the driver was standing by the car as if he had been waiting on me forever when I was right on time.

"Thank you," I politely said after he opened the door for me. Before I was even able to get comfortable in the backseat Kennedy went right in.

"I love how punctual you've become. I was getting worried for a minute but then you came out right on time."

"Kennedy, when you tell me to be ready aren't I always?"

"Yes, I just want to make sure you don't fall back into bad habits."

"I'm positive you won't ever let that happen. So what exactly are we attending tonight?"

"You remember Marcus Powell?"

"Oh yeah, the big time executive over at Lionsgate."

"Exactly. Well he's become a client of mine

and the guy who is overseeing the New York office is having a very intimate dinner at his penthouse so of course I have to attend. It's only going to be a handful of people there so it's good for you to rub shoulders with these powerful individuals. Believe it or not the more they see your face at these sorts of shindigs the better it is for your career. Never forget this business is all about building the right relationships.

"I get it and that's why I'm here."

"And of course we're not going to stay that long. It's much better for people to hate to see you go then to say you stayed too long."

"Good, that means I'll still have time to see Kirk tonight."

"Kirk, I thought he was just a friend and Michael was your man."

"Michael is my man and I've become fond of spending time with Kirk. We have fun together."

"What kind of fun?"

"Get your mind out the gutter, Kennedy. Not that kind of fun."

"Don't blame me. Kirk McNight is about the closest thing to perfection you can get. You would be crazy not to have some fun with him."

"Lets move on to another topic, like lets discuss your love life. How's that coming along?

"It's not. I made a deal with myself that I will not get involved in a relationship until I've become a successful businesswoman. And with Diamond and I starting this company together I think it might happen even sooner than I thought."

"I hope so. Maybe it's not my place to say this but you work way too much. It's nothing wrong with working hard but you need to enjoy life too."

"Blair, not everybody has a rich boyfriend taking care of them. I have real responsibilities and if I don't take care of myself then I'm fucked."

"I understand and so you know I'm striving for that same independence that you are."

"I know and I apologize for taking that jab at you."

"It's okay, because you're right. I got myself in a fucked up situation and I can't seem to get myself out of it."

"You don't have to answer this question if you don't want to."

"Ask me, I'll answer it."

"Why do you stay with Michael? I know I haven't met him but it seems every time you talk about him it's painful."

"You know how many times I've asked myself that exact same question."

"What did you come up with?"

"I do love him and I guess I'm determined to make him love me back."

"You do know you can't make anybody love you."

"I know but the thing is I do believe Michael loves me the best way he knows how."

"We're here and I want you to go inside with a smile on your face and not this heavy bullshit. How about we make a deal that we'll finish discussing this over drinks tomorrow."

"Deal."

"Great, now I need you to put on your superstar smile and lets go."

"You got it."

When we entered the penthouse the first thing I noticed was the crystal and gold trim chandelier that was hanging in the huge marble foyer. It was gorgeous and I became transfixed on it. I couldn't stop staring until Kennedy nudged my arm for me to come on. We followed the maid to a room where a few people were talking in the den and others were sitting down watching the news. It really was a small intimate gathering.

"Oh fuck, what is she doing here," Kennedy said in a low voice.

"Who?" I was looking at the handful of people in the room and was trying to figure out who Kennedy was talking about.

"Darcy, hi, it's good to see you."

"It's good to see you too although surprising. Who invited you?"

"Kennedy, it's great to finally meet you in person," a middle aged, heavyset black man with a jolly smile, said extending his hand out to Kennedy.

"John, it's great to see you too and you're home is immaculate."

"Thank you. I'm glad you could make it."

"I wouldn't have missed it for anything. This is Blair and..."

"Darcy, her boss," Darcy jumped in and said cutting Kennedy off.

"Nice to meet you both." I liked how John remained cool and calm although you could tell he was a little thrown off like all of us were by Darcy's brashness.

"Kennedy, I'm going to go speak to a friend of mine but lets sit down and talk before you leave."

"Will do."

"What the hell is going on, Kennedy?"

"What are you talking about?"

"Cut the bullshit. I'm not new to this game I invented it. Are you cutting deals behind my back?"

"No I'm not and I don't think it's appropriate for us to have this conversation here."

"We'll have this conversation any damn where I see fit."

"Can you keep your voice down people are starting to stare."

"Excuse me, I'm going to get a drink. Can I bring you something back, Kennedy?"

"Yes, bring back some champagne. Thanks." In the short period of time it took me to get two glasses of champagne from one of the servers, a full fledged argument was about to erupt and a face I knew very well was now a part of it.

"Michael, what are you doing here?"

"That's Michael, your Michael?" Kennedy questioned with a puzzled look on her face.

"No he's my Michael and who the hell are you," Darcy spit.

"Hold up," I said, putting both my hands up. I swallowed hard before I could say another word. "Do you know this woman?"

"Of course he knows me. I'm his woman and I'm asking you again, who are you?"

"Blair, what are you doing here? Why aren't you home."

"You mean home waiting for you? This is who you've been seeing behind my back?"

"Who the hell do you think you are? He hasn't been seeing me behind your back I'm his woman and you must be some little plaything."

"Darcy, that's enough. You need to go sit down somewhere while I talk to Blair."

"Michael, you can't be serious."

"Yes I am. Now excuse me while I speak to Blair."

"Who did you come here with?"

"Kennedy, but does any of that matter? You've

been seeing another woman behind my back."

"Stop, don't do this here."

"Do what, show emotions? I forgot I'm supposed to be cold like you. I'm done trying to please you. Go be with Darcy or whatever other woman you want, I'm done."

"You'll never be done with me," Michael stated, grabbing my arm.

"I used to think that too but not any more."

"Where are you going to go? I'm all you have."

"That's where you're wrong. You finally overplayed your hand."

"You're hurt right now and you're saying things you don't mean but..."

"Omigoodness! Turn that up," I heard Kennedy yell out.

"Let go of me...what's wrong, Kennedy."

"Look," she said pointing towards the television. Someone turned up the volume and I felt like my heart was jumping out my chest. There was footage of Diamond being escorted out of the high-rise apartment she lived at on Central Park West with her hands behind her back in handcuffs.

Diamond O' Toole the girlfriend of New York Knicks superstar Cameron Robinson was arrested and charged with conspiracy to commit murder and drug trafficking. At this time federal agents aren't giving out any further details but we will keep you posted as this story develops.

"What the fuck is going on, Kennedy?"

"I don't know but there has to be some sort of mistake and we're going to get to the bottom of it. Let's go."

"Blair, where are you going?" Michael said, gripping my arm tightly.

"To find out what's going on with my friend."

"I'm an attorney let me come with you so I can help."

"I don't want you anywhere near me so let me go," I huffed, jerking my arm away from Michal.

"Blair, you're going to regret walking away from me."

"Then so be it but I have more important things to do. Like go help a real friend, something you know nothing about." As Kennedy and I rushed out to try and figure out what was going on with Diamond, I wanted to believe everything we heard on the news was nothing but lies. If anything happened to her I wouldn't know what to do. Diamond was more than a best friend to me she was like a sister. And for that reason alone, I made up my mind I would do whatever was necessary to make sure she came back home to us.

Diamond

This some bullshit right here! I thought, shaking my head as I stood in the corner of my holding cell. I refused to sit my ass down because I had foolishly convinced myself that I was going home tonight. In reality I wouldn't know when and if I was going home until a lawyer got me in front of a judge and I had a bail hearing. It would take a miracle for some shit like that to happen tonight and the way my luck was going, it wasn't in the cards.

Drug trafficking...conspiracy to commit murder...these motherfuckers ain't playing I thought to myself. I couldn't help but wonder how I went from relaxing in a lavish penthouse Cameron got for me and Destiny, to being handcuffed and dragged to a fuckin' jail cell. I kept shaking my head wondering how it all went wrong and it led me back to one person...that nigga Tech.

When I had my suspicions about Rico's friend Parish, I called the one person I always did who I knew could handle shit without any hiccups. Tech had taken care of so much dirt for me in the past and I always hit him off properly. It had been a beneficial relationship for both of us without any problems that is until now. I thought back to that night when Cameron and I had sex for the first time. I called Tech after I realized I had missed his call but he didn't answer. I assumed everything was straight but I never heard back from him. I figured he was trying to lay low like he would typically do when he had to handle some ruthless type shit for me. Or I thought he had quickly picked up another job from somebody else that was keeping him busy and he would be in touch. Tech services were always in demand because he was supposed to be one of the best at what he did but now it was looking like I would have to give him a new title...snitch.

"Your attorney is here to see you," I heard the guard call out, shaking me out of my thoughts.

"My attorney," I mumbled in a low tone. It was crazy because when they first brought me in these fucks had come up with all sorts of reasons why I had to wait to make a phone call so I didn't even have a chance to call an attorney. At this point, of course I was completely baffled but relieved at the same time that I had representation.

"Diamond O'Toole, it's a pleasure," the tall lanky man with salt & pepper hair and a thick mustache said, extending his hand. "I'm Miles

Hamilton...your attorney. Please have a seat."

"First, let me be clear, I am beyond thrilled to have an attorney here to represent me but of course I have to ask who hired you? I haven't been able to make a phone call, so I'm trying to figure out what's going on."

"Cameron Robinson has retained me to represent you."

"Cameron," I said, as my mouth dropped. "But he's on the road. He has like three or four games on the west coast how would he know about me being arrested?"

"When the girlfriend of a major NBA player is arrested for drug trafficking and conspiracy to commit murder, I'm sure you realize that's going to be breaking news on every major media outlet."

"You're telling me this is all over the news?"

"That's exactly what I'm telling you." At that moment I was completely mortified. I wanted to crawl up into a small ball and just roll away. "But luckily for you, you have a boyfriend that's very concerned about your well being. I was able to pull in a few favors and I will get you in front of a judge tonight."

"Are you serious?"

"Very. You'll learn quickly that I never play when it comes to the law." Part of me was praising the Lord that I was becoming a recipient of a much-needed miracle, but the other part of me kept thinking about my mother. She had to see the news and if she didn't somebody definitely called her about my dilemma. *Fuck! She is probably going crazy!* I screamed to myself. If I could find one silver lining in this bullshit was that Destiny had been with my mother when I got arrested so she didn't have to see when those police officers clanked those handcuffs around my wrists.

"Do you think you'll be able to get me out tonight?" I finally asked after my mind had wondered off thinking about my mother and Destiny.

"I'm very confident. You're facing some serious charges so I'm sure the bail will be set high. But Cameron made it clear he would cover whatever amount was issued by the judge so you should be fine."

"Do you know how these charges came about?"

"I haven't gotten any of that information yet. The state seems to be trying to play this close to the vest but trust me, by tomorrow morning, afternoon at the latest I'll have many more details."

"That's good to know. I want to know where these charges are stemming from."

"Of course you do. Are you ready to see the judge?"

"As ready as I'll ever be. But umm...don't you have something you want to ask me?"

"I think we covered everything for now. We will get into a deeper conversation when I know exactly what the state's case is."

"Don't you want to know if the charges are true...if I'm guilty of what they're accusing me of?"

"Only if that's how you plan to plea. Is that what you're going to do...plead guilty? Because if that's the case tell me now so I can try to get you the best plea deal possible. If not then as far as the law is concerned you're innocent until proven guilty... that's my only concern, what the law states and how those laws apply to my client. So are you ready?"

"Yes, I'm ready," I stated standing up. For the first time since I was read my rights a boost of confidence shot through me. It was amazing how a high priced attorney could make you go from feeling defeated to almost invincible in a matter of minutes...the magic of words.

Kennedy

When I arrived at Diamond's high-rise there were paparazzi and news reporters posted outside her building waiting for that front page shot. I hurried inside surprised by all the hoopla. There was extra security inside the building and besides them calling upstairs to confirm I could come up like they did normally, this time I had to show ID.

"Kennedy, thanks so much for coming," Diamond said, when she opened the door.

"Of course!" I stated closing the door. "When Blair and I came down to the police station last night and they said you had already been released we were so relieved. We came straight over but you weren't here."

"Yeah, I spent the night at my mother's crib. I wanted to see Destiny, because I knew she would need to stay at my mom's place until things settled down."

"I know what you mean. It's a jungle out there."

"Tell me about it. They had me come in through this secret back entrance so I could bypass all that bullshit. They out there waiting for Cameron. He's supposed to be back from the team's road trip today and they so fuckin' thirsty to get a photo of him coming to see me." I could see the stress all on Diamond's face when she mentioned Cameron. I didn't want to bombard Diamond with questions because I could only imagine how overwhelmed she must've been but I wanted her to know that I was here for her.

"Diamond, it's going to all work out. I know this must be a huge mistake. Why else would they let you out on bail so quickly on a conspiracy to commit murder charge and drug trafficking? This will all be over with very soon."

Instead of reassuring me that I was right, Diamond simply sat down on the couch and gave me no response. Her mind seemed to be somewhere else. I was about to say something but then she looked up at me and spoke.

"It's not a mistake, Kennedy."

"Excuse me?" That's all I could get out before my mouthed dropped.

"Meaning the charges are going to stick it's not a mistake but what they're accusing me of isn't true, it's all lies."

"Well of course they're lies," I said, breathing a sigh of relief. "You had me confused there for a minute when you said it wasn't a mistake, but I understand what you meant now. Of course the state is going to try and make the charges stick but once they realize they have no evidence trust me the charges will be dropped."

"I hope you're right but you never know."

"You got out on bail didn't you!"

"Yeah, but that's because Cameron got me a big time high powered lawyer. He pulled some strings and he posted the bail. He has been so good to Destiny and me. I just don't deserve all his kindness."

"Of course you do! Diamond, you're the most generous person I know. You don't deserve what is happening to you and Cameron knows it, that's why he did everything possible to get you out of jail. Somebody is clearly setting you up and I wouldn't be surprised if it's your bitter ass baby daddy Rico. I mean where would anybody get the idea that you're selling drugs? That's what he does not you."

"Maybe you're right, I don't know. Only thing I'm sure of is that I have to find a way to get out of this. I can't go to jail, Kennedy. My daughter needs me. The thought of being locked away and not able to raise Destiny is too much to even fathom."

"Get those thoughts out your mind because it's never going to happen," I tried to reassure her. The tears were swelling up in Diamond's eyes and it broke my heart to see her so scared. Diamond was always the one so in control and with all the great ideas to make shit work. To see her vulnerable had me worried.

"Kennedy, it's not that simple."

"What do you mean?" I asked, going over to sit down next to Diamond on the couch.

"I have some..." before Diamond could complete the sentence we both turned around because we heard the front door opening, a few seconds later Cameron walked in.

"Baby, you're back," Diamond stood up and said before walking over to Cameron.

"I came here straight from the airport," he said dropping his luggage and then reaching out to hug her. She laid her head in Cameron's chest and held on to him like he was the only one who could protect her from all the chaos that had entered her life.

"I'm sure you all need to talk. I'll call you later on, Diamond."

"Ok, thanks again for coming by."

"You know I'm always here for you. Call me if you need me. Good to see you, Cameron," I smiled before heading out. I stood in the hallway for a few minutes thinking about my conversation with Diamond. I was so happy that Cameron was back because she needed all the support she could get. Then I thought about the new PR Company we were supposed to start together. I didn't want to seem selfish, but I wanted her to get all this court stuff behind her as quickly as possible. Although I never doubted it but now that I heard it out of her own mouth that she was innocent, I was ready to move forward with our new business venture. Of course I would give Diamond some time to get things together because her energy would need to go towards beating her case. I realized I would have to deal with my piece of shit boss Darcy for a little while longer, but I had no worries. There was no doubt in my mind Diamond would have the mayhem in her life under control sooner rather than later.

Blair

As I was packing up my belongings I heard a key in the door and I knew it had to be Michael. I had no interest in seeing him after what happened last night at the party but the encounter was unavoidable. When he came in I kept packing, not even acknowledging his presence.

"What are doing?"

"I think it's pretty obvious."

"Blair, stop being dramatic and stop packing. We both know you're not going any where."

"You don't get it. I'm done, Michael! You've been cheating on me for I don't know how long and besides that you're not even interested in my life."

"What life...you don't have a life. Your life consist of me taking care of you and I do a very good job doing so."

"That's all over with. I don't need you to take care of me any longer, I can take care of myself."

"It takes money to live, Blair and with the

lifestyle I have you accustomed to, it takes a lot and that's something you simply don't have."

"I don't care. I'm going to stay with Kennedy and I'll continue to work on building my career. I might have to struggle, but it'll be worth it if I can get the hell away from you."

"You want to play tough...I'll show you just how tough it's going to be. For starters you can stop packing."

"I told you I'm leaving!"

"I know and you are leaving but you won't be taking anything out of this apartment except for the hand me down clothes I found you in." I swallowed hard trying to regain my composure. I was stunned by what Michael just said.

"You can't be serious."

"Dead serious. You want out then get out but you won't benefit from anything I've done for you if you're not with me. It's that simple."

"I've been through enough with you. Don't do this."

"Then stay. I know you want to."

"What about Darcy?"

"What about her?"

"Are you going to stop seeing her?"

"Here's the thing, Blair. Darcy and any other woman are irrelevant to our relationship. You are my woman and as long as you're my woman you'll never have to want for anything. But what you won't do is question me. Know your place and stay in it. If you would just follow that simple rule our relationship would go a lot smoother."

"Fuck you, Michael! I'm not that same pathetic girl you found who worked at a diner."

"Well that's where you'll be going back to if you walk out that door and leave me."

"Then so be it. I rather get down on my knees and scrub dirty floors then deal with mental abuse from you," I said, trying not to cry. I hated that my anger was getting the best of me but I couldn't hold back the tears.

"Baby, don't cry," Michael said, taking his finger and wiping away my tears.

"Stop," I demanded, moving back away from him.

Michael stepped closer and whispered in my ear, "You know you belong to me," as he slid his hand down my blouse circling my nipple with his fingers before clasping the tip. He then began sprinkling my neck with kisses, before I knew it we were lying down on the Persian silk rug naked and Michael's tongue was seducing my clit. My mind was fighting against the temptation but the desires of my body won and I found myself opening my legs wider welcoming Michael to make love to me.

As his tongue hypnotized me he then switched up and let his dick take over. I couldn't control my moans of pleasure as Michael kept going deeper and deeper inside of me. "Don't ever say you're leaving me, do you understand?" I heard Michael ask between my oohs and ahhs. "Answer me," he demanded as he continued twisting my insides out.

"Yes, I understand."

"Are you sure?"

"Yes, I'm sure," I called out, willing to say whatever he wanted so he could keep stroking as he was hitting my G spot. My hips and ass were pumping faster wanting to feel all of Michael inside of me. "Oh, baby I'm about to cum!" I cried out.

"I know," Michael stated staring directly in my eyes before pulling out.

"Baby, what are you doing," I sighed, reaching out to Michael trying to pull him back inside of me. "Why did you stop? I was about to cum. Put it back inside," I begged touching his still rock hard manhood. Instead he started jackin' off in front of me. Before long he made himself cum and I just watched in disbelief.

"I wanted you to understand what else you'll be missing if you decide to leave me. You'll have no money but more than that we both know, nobody has ever fucked you as good as me."

As much as part of me hated Michael he was right. I did like the way he took care of me, but I loved the way he fucked me. He was able to make my body feel ways that no other man had ever come close to doing. It was like he had the blueprint to every spot that got me hot. "Why do you do this to me?"

"Because I love you."

"This isn't love. I don't know what to call what we have but you don't love me."

"Yes I do. If I didn't I would let you go."

"Then why can't you be true to me?"

"I have to take a shower. You can unpack your stuff while I'm doing so," Michael said, not even bothering to answer my question. I laid on the rug in the fetal position disgusted with myself. I was so weak for a man that treated me like shit. I wanted to break free but I seemed to have a need to stay with Michael more. I hated the hold he had on me, but I couldn't seem to shake it.

Diamond

"Baby, I know I've said it over and over again but thank you for getting me the attorney and putting up the bail money," I said as we lay in the bed. We had just made love and I was snuggled under Cameron feeling as if he was my protector.

"Diamond, I'll always make sure you're straight. You my girl and we a team, we'll beat this case together."

"I hope you're right."

"Of course I am. You a drug dealer, ordering a murder...that shit don't even sound right. I know you. You not even capable of no bullshit like that. Personally, I think yo' baby daddy got popped and then he tried to spin it and put that shit on you."

"I don't know about that."

"It makes sense. You told me when you all were together he was selling and as far as you know he never stopped. Plus the two of you don't get along. If he got into some trouble you would be an easy target."

"Maybe, but as much as I dislike Rico and he dislikes me I don't think he would stoop that low."

"See what I mean. You are too sweet for your own good. If not yo' baby daddy then who?"

"I have no idea but we'll figure it out." I hated lying to Cameron. There was nothing to figure out because all the charges were true. I had a good idea who was behind my downfall and it wasn't Rico. It had to be the dude that I hired to get rid of Parish snake ass. I wanted to reach out to Tech but if I was correct then the cops had to have him under surveillance and probably was waiting and wishing that I called him so whatever I said would help corroborate the story he told them. But if they were expecting that they would have to keep waiting. But I did want to speak to one person that might be able to shed light on some things and that was Rico.

"Baby, I'ma go to my mother's house for a few hours and spend time with Destiny."

"I know it's hard being away from her but hopefully this shit will die down soon."

"That would be nice but I have a feeling that it's not."

"How 'bout I go with you to your mother's. We'll take Destiny to the park and go get some ice cream. She'll love that."

"I know you're trying to lift my spirits and I love you for that but I don't want to take Destiny out.

You know the paparazzi will be all over us especially if they see us with you."

"Fuck them muthafuckers! They not gon' make us hide out and stop living our lives."

"Not forever but right now I just want a little bit of peace. So let me go to my mother's house alone...ok?"

"If that's what you want but you know I got your back."

"I know. I'm so lucky to have you," I said, kissing Cameron on his soft lips. As I straddled Cameron ready for us to make love again, my body was here but my mind was someplace else. I had to figure a way out of this nightmare. Cameron had put me on this pedestal as some sweet young single mother that he wanted to save and take care of. If he found out that I was really this calculating, somewhat ruthless drug dealer he would hate me and I couldn't blame him.

When I got in the car the first thing I did was call Rico. He picked up on the fourth ring. "What up," he answered.

"I need you to meet me at my mother's house in thirty minutes."

"For what?'

"Just come. I need to talk to you about something."

"Is everything ok with Destiny?"

"Yes, she's fine."

"Then why can't you say whatever it is over the phone?"

"Because I can't. Now are you gonna come?"

"Yeah...yeah...yeah, I'll be there," he said hanging up. The first thing I wondered after Rico hung up was if he had heard about my arrest. I was thinking he hadn't since he didn't mention it. Rico wasn't the type to watch the news but I figured somebody would've hit him up about it by now or maybe the streets weren't yet talking. Regardless I needed to lock eyes with Rico and find out what he knew about Parish.

When I pulled up to my mom's crib, Rico was already there, sitting outside on the front stool waiting for me. I found a parking space right in front of my mom's building and I got out quickly anxious to pick Rico's brain.

"What up ma," he said standing up as I approached.

"Does Destiny know you're here?"

"Nah, I did knock on the door but ya mom didn't answer. I don't know if that they not home or your moms just don't want to see me. We both know I ain't her favorite person."

"They must've stepped out. They might be

back by the time we finish."

"Finish...so what you call me over here for?"

"Remember I told you I was robbed awhile back?"

"Yeah..and?"

"Well, I heard it was your friend Parish that did it?"

"Huh?" he asked with his face screwed up.

"You heard me right. I heard yo' man Parish was the one that ran up in my spot."

"Is that why you put that hit out on him?" I stood there not saying anything for a second. "Yeah, you thought I ain't hear about that shit. I know yo' triflin' ass was arrested over that shit. I just didn't want to clown you over the phone. I wanted to say that shit to yo' face."

"Say what?"

"That yo' ass is going down," he snarled walking closer towards me.

"So it don't bother you that yo' man walked up in my crib with a gun and robbed me?"

"That nigga didn't do no shit like that!"

"Yes the fuck he did!"

"You a lie! You tryna pin that shit on him 'cause you know he my people. But it ain't gon' work. You tryna play like you a boss gon get you ten to twenty-five behind bars and yo' little rich basketball boyfriend ain't gon' be able to do a damn thing about it," he mocked with a sinister laugh.

"You such a bitchass nigga. I'm the mother of yo' child and you want to see me locked up. You want your daughter raised without her mother all because you wanna act like a scorned broad!"

"Fuck you, Diamond! It ain't my fault you wanted to be out in these streets like you a nigga pushing drugs like you a kingpin."

"Oh I get it. You mad 'cause I learned how to do it better than you. You can't take that I was making more money than you out in these streets. Yo' ego all fucked up. I wouldn't be surprised if you were in on that robbery."

"As foul as I think you are I would never cosign on no nigga comin' up in the crib my daughter rest her head at and stickin' you up. Like I said Parish didn't have nothing to do wit' that shit and because of you that nigga could be dead right now."

"I only got two things to say to you and then this conversation is over. Yo' snake ass friend Parish did rob me and as much as you're praying for my downfall I am a boss and will beat these charges."

Kennedy

"Just a minute," I called out when I heard somebody at the front door. "I wonder who that could be?" I asked out loud right before I looked through the peephole.

"Hey," Blair said, standing in front of the door with an awkward smile on her face.

"What are you doing here and what's up with the bags?"

"You said I could stay with you unless you changed your mind.'

"That was two weeks ago and from our last conversation you're the one that changed your mind."

"Well I changed it back, if the offer still stands."

"Come on in," I said, standing off to the side so Blair could walk past me. "Dare I ask what happened that made you decide to actually pack your bags and leave Michael," I questioned as I closed the door.

"These last couple weeks has been the same

as always and I decided I had to stop being afraid to make it without him."

"You sure this ain't a temporary move because you didn't bring much stuff," I stated, looking down at Blair's two duffel bags.

"Michael told me I could only leave with what I came with and that wasn't much. It feels good though, it's like I'm starting from scratch."

"That you are but I'ma have to get you some clothes. I have a slew of potential gigs for you and I need you to look the part when you go for these interviews."

"I feel you but until then we have to work with what I got."

"Don't trip I got a homegirl that can hook you up with some clothes asap."

"You sure?"

"Most definitely! She's a stylist and I always get her and her clients passes to the best parties/ events so she stay owing me a favor."

"You're the best, Kennedy...thanks so much."

"You're *my* client and when you win I win plus the faster I can get you some real money gigs the quicker I can get you out my crib," I joked. "But seriously, you're welcome to stay as long as you like."

"You mean that?"

"Yes! I'm proud of you because honestly I didn't think you would ever get enough strength to make that break from Michael. He seemed to have such a strong hold on you."

"He does...I mean he did but I'm ready to do me."

"That's the attitude I like. Now get yourself situated because I have to go to work. I'm going to call you in a couple hours and update you on a few things I got lined up. I'm also going to hit up my homegirl, so she can either come over here or you meet her at her spot so we can get this wardrobe situation under control."

"Sounds good. I'll just wait for your phone call."

On my way to the office everything that I had to make happen for Blair was running through my mind. Although she was putting up a tough girl front I could tell she was debating in her mind if she made the right decision leaving Michael. I wanted to secure a hot gig for her soon to give her self-esteem a boost, so she would know that leaving him was the right decision. As thoughts were rambling on in my head my cell vibrating interrupted them. "Hey, Tish what's up?"

"Hey! I just wanted to give you a heads us that the Skee Patron video is finally about to drop. It premiers tomorrow."

"Yo, I need that in my life! That shit got pushed back so many times I was starting to think it was never coming out."

"I know…I know. The label was just trying to give him the perfect setup and now they feel it's the right time."

"Great! I appreciate you letting me know."

"You know I got you." When I hung up with Tish I felt so good. I had been counting on that video to give Blair some real exposure so I could build off that to get her more gigs but I had been stressing that was never gonna happen. But getting this call from Tish changed all that. The first thing I was going to do when I got to the office was write up a press release about Blair's debut and send that shit out.

"Good morning, Tammy!" I sashayed into the office with an extra pep in my step.

"Aren't you in a good mood," she said, sounding surprised.

"Yeah, I have a lot to feel good about. Listen, I'm working on something very important so you'll be making a lot of phone calls for me today."

"No problem, just tell me what you need me to do."

"I'm going to type up the pitch letter for you so when you make the calls you know exactly what to say."

"I'm ready."

"Good. So start pulling up all the urban media contacts so you'll be ready to pull the trigger as soon as I say go."

I sat down and typed out the pitch letter first so Tammy could immediately get on making phone calls and while she was doing that I could prepare the press release. In between doing that I reached out to the stylist so she could meet up with Blair. As I was in the middle of getting my grove on and poppin' I felt a dark cloud swoop through the office.

"Kennedy, I need to speak to you," I heard Darcy say as I was putting the final touches on Blair's press release. I hit save on the Word Document and followed Darcy to her office.

"What can I do for you, Darcy?"

"I just received a very interesting phone call."

"Really...what was it about?'

"That skank I saw you at the party with a few weeks ago."

"You're going to have to be more specific because I don't hang with skanks so I have no idea who you're talking about."

"You know exactly who I'm referring to." I stood mute as if I was clueless. I wasn't going to make the rant Darcy was about to go on easy for her. "That Blair chick."

"Oh, Blair what about her?"

"A media outlet wanted to congratulate me on getting my client a feature in Skee Patron's new music video. Of course I didn't know what the hell they were talking about because I would never represent a nobody like her."

"Well, clearly she isn't a nobody since you're getting a call about her," I shot back. I watched as Darcy shifted in her chair, annoyed by my response.

"The point is why would a media outlet think she is my client?"

"I have no idea. You should've asked whoever called you."

"I did but they seemed clueless."

"So am I but she seems to be on her way to being the new it girl, maybe that's why the person assumed Blair was your client. You are known to always have the newest and hottest clients."

"There is nothing hot about that Blair bitch."

"Darcy, your jealousy is starting to show. You always told me that you should never let your personal feelings get in the way of business."

"I have no interest in Blair. Yeah, she might be in Skee's new video but her career won't go anywhere after that. I can recognize a star and she just doesn't have what it takes."

"I hear you. Is that all you wanted to discuss with me?"

"Yes, that's all for now...so you can go," Darcy snapped, anxious to dismiss me. I found it humorous that Darcy was throwing so much shade at Blair. All her words did was motivate me to go harder. I was more determined than ever to make Blair a star.

Blair

"Congratulations!" I heard the familiar voice say over the phone.

"Thanks so much."

"How does it feel to be a star?"

"Whatever! I'm not a star yet."

"Yeah, but you're on the way. I had been wondering when that video was going to be released and when I saw it last night my mouth dropped. You looked amazing."

"Thanks, Kirk. It's crazy because you were right there with me when it was happening."

"I know and the final cut came out even better than I thought it would. That director did his thing. So how do you feel?"

"I feel great! I have never got so many phone calls in my life. It seems like everybody and they mother has seen it."

"Yo' that's Skee Patron. Everybody check for that dudes music. That was an excellent look!"

"Yeah, it seems that way. Kennedy did her

thing making that happen."

"She sure did...and you delivered. Can I take you out to dinner tonight to celebrate or do you already have plans?"

"Actually I don't. I would love to celebrate with you."

"Cool, I'll pick you up around 7?"

"That works, but I'm staying with a friend so I'll text you my new address."

"So you moved?"

"Yep."

"Does that mean you finally gave homeboy his walking papers?"

"Something like that."

"Smart move. Maybe now you'll finally give me a chance."

"You never know."

"No pressure, babe...I'll see tonight." As soon as I hung up with Kirk, Kennedy called.

"What's up Kennedy!"

"You...you...you and more you! Girl, my phone is blowing up over you. I knew that video would work magic for your career and I love when I'm right."

"Are you serious?"

"Yes, I got so many different offers but we have to be very strategic about what we have you do next. I don't want to have you in all sorts of bullshit just for a check. Skee Patron is a top notch artist so we have to move accordingly."

"I totally get that."

"When I get home tonight we can go over some ideas I have."

"Kirk invited me to have a celebratory dinner with him tonight but I can cancel so we can go over your ideas."

"Hell no! Are you crazy! I almost forgot about Kirk due to all that bullshit you've been going through with Michael. Dinner with Kirk McKnight is way more important than anything I'll be talking about tonight."

"You're so silly."

"I'm so serious. As a matter of fact do you know where you all are having dinner?"

"No, not yet."

"As soon as you find out let me know."

"Why, are you coming through?"

"Not! I'm going to call up one of my photographer friends so he can get some pics of you all out on your date. With the video you're in premiering this is perfect. People will think every hot nigga doing big things right now is checking for you. This is the type of shit blogs and magazines live for."

"If you think it'll help the cause lets do it."

"Excellent. So find out where Kirk is taking you to dinner and I'll handle the rest."

"I'm on it." When I hung up with Kennedy, I got to thinking. I felt kinda bad using Kirk for a photo op but as the same time I trusted Kennedy's opinion. Plus things were different I was now on my own. I no longer had Michael as a financial crutch and I had to do whatever was necessary to make it, and if that meant letting Kennedy stage a photo then so be it.

When we arrived at Park Avenue Autumn on East 63rd Street, the photographer was ready and waiting to take our pic. I tried to act surprised and annoyed at first but then I realized if I kept frowning my face Kennedy wouldn't have any good pictures of me to circulate to the press.

"I can't believe the paparazzi came over to the East side to get a pic of us going into a restaurant. That shit crazy," Kirk commented as he held the door open for me.

"I know, but I guess that comes with the territory of being a superstar NBA player," I smiled, trying to throw any suspicion off of me.

When we got inside Kirk didn't even have to give his name, it was pretty obvious who he was. The hostess immediately took us to our table. After we were sitting down for no more than ten minutes, I spotted the photographer inside trying to take more pictures. I wanted to cringe from embarrassment. Kirk noticed the expression on my face and turned around to see what had me looking so pissed off.

"This muthafucka can't be serious." Kirk stood up from his chair about to walk in the direction of the photographer but he was already being escorted out by management. I was almost positive that he got the shot he wanted so he probably didn't care.

"I'm sorry about that," I said, when Kirk sat back down.

"What you sorry for it ain't yo' fault that people so damn disrespectful. We trying to have a quiet dinner and this dumb fuck want to snap some pictures. How desperate can you be," he continued, shaking his head.

"I know what you mean," I nodded, taking a sip of my water.

"Enough about him tonight is all about you. You got the streets talking. Everybody wants to know who that girl is in Skee's video and she's sitting here with me."

"Stop! You're gonna make me blush."

"I'm simply telling it like it is. I was surprised though that you were able to have dinner with me tonight. I assumed you would be celebrating with your man."

"You know I told you that Michael doesn't really support or care about the career I'm trying to build. But that no longer matters."

"Why is that?"

"Because we broke up."

"When did that happen?"

"It's been in the works for awhile but things went completely downhill a couple weeks ago. "

"It must've been pretty bad."

"Yeah it was. I found out he was cheating

on me and he basically told me I had to accept it. That man has zero respect for me and I knew if I didn't make a change things were going to stay the same."

"So you walked away."

"Yep. I'm staying with Kennedy. She's being extremely supportive. Honestly, if she hadn't told me I could live with her, I probably would've stayed," I admitted, lowering my head in shame.

"Blair, everybody needs support. That's nothing for you to feel bad about. The point is you left and I'm for one, is very happy about it. Maybe now you'll give a nigga a chance."

"You're so silly."

"I'm serious. I told you that if you gave me a chance I would make you happy. I want you to give me that opportunity. Will you?" Kirk reached over and took my hand. He slid his fingers in between mine and stared at me.

"I would like that. After everything I've been through with Michael, I do still believe in love. I want to see what can happen with us." Right at that moment our waitress brought over the bottle of champagne Kirk ordered. After pouring our glasses, Kirk lifted his up.

"Let's give a toast to new beginnings."

"To new beginnings," I repeated as we clicked our glasses.

Diamond

"The prosecutor is building a case to charge you with Queen Pin status," my attorney said as I sat across from him at his office on Lexington Avenue.

"Are you sure?'

"I wouldn't be telling you if I wasn't."

"What evidence do they have?"

"It's a sealed indictment so I don't have all the information but I should know more soon."

"For the charges they are trying to make stick what do you think?"

"It's only speculation, but I'm assuming they have an informant that's willing to testify against you. I would think they are working towards getting others to do the same."

"How many years am I facing?"

"Twenty-five unless you cooperate and take a plea."

"I'm not a snitch."

"So I'm assuming you want to fight the case."

"Of course. Do you think you can beat it?"

"I'm still not sure what their case consist of but they must be somewhat confident based on the charges they're bringing against you."

This isn't happening to me. Twenty-five years behind bars...this can't be my life I thought to myself as I began pacing my attorney's office. My palms were sweaty and my heart was racing. There had to be a way out of this but what I wasn't sure.

"I can't go to jail."

"I'll do everything in my power to make sure that doesn't happen but I can't promise you anything."

"Please don't discuss my case with Cameron."

"What we discuss is privileged. Just because Cameron is footing the bill doesn't change that. But your situation might turn dire," he stressed, so you may want to prepare Cameron for that."

"You're making it sound like we already loss," I barked.

"I'm not saying that, it's only a suggestion. It's my job to lay all the cards on the table."

"I'll take care of Cameron you just focus on beating this case." I grabbed my purse and made my exit. Going to jail wasn't an option. I knew what had to happen and I was prepared to do it. I just needed to make sure I had all the facts before I made my move.

When I got in my car I immediately placed a phone call and I prayed the person would answer.

"This better be important." I breathed a sigh of relief when I heard his voice on the other end of the phone.

"It is. I need to see you."

"I don't think that's a good idea."

"Please...this is about my life. I need your help."

"I'll call you back in an hour," is all he said before hanging up the phone. I put my head down on the steering wheel and a tear rolled down my cheek. The very moment I was trying to get my life right shit had to hit the fan. I had a great man, I was about to start this new business with Kennedy and become legit but now I was facing twenty-five years in jail. There was no way I would let Destiny be raised by her father especially since he was cheering for my demise.

In the middle of me contemplating what the future held for me I remembered I was supposed to meet Blair for lunch. I looked at my watch and then sent her a text message since I knew I would be late. As I drove off headed towards Times Square, I felt I was having hot flashes and the walls were closing in on me. Then I just started praying.

"Dear God please forgive me. I've made so many bad choices and I'm about to make some more. I know I'm not worthy and it's only by your Grace I'm still standing but I beg you to help me get through this dark time in my life." I wasn't sure if my prayer would work, but I mos def needed a miracle if I could manage to finagle my way out of this mess. The hole

I had dug was so deep I had no choice but to finish what I started.

Blair was sitting at the bar when I arrived at Cava inside the Intercontinental in Times Square. "Hey, so sorry I'm late," I said giving her a hug.

"No worries. I'm on my second Bellini. I think this place might make the best ones in the city."

"I know. That's why I wanted to have lunch here. I need the bartender to go ahead and bring me about three off the gate," I huffed waving my hand to get her attention.

"Stressful day."

"Make that stressful weeks but today the final nail in the coffin."

"Why what happened?" Blair turned towards me and the concerned poured out of her eyes.

"I met with my attorney before coming here and lets just say he didn't have very encouraging news."

"Really?" Blair said, sounding shocked. "I don't understand. I figured those charges had to be bogus and would never stick."

"Blair, you know we go all the way back to hopscotch days so I'm going to keep things super straight with you. But I also expect for this conversation to never leave this restaurant. Once I tell you this you have to act like I never did...follow me." Her eyes widened in anticipation of what I had to say.

"Of course. Whatever we discuss will stay between us. I promise."

"I appreciate that." I was relieved to finally have someone that I trusted to confide in. I felt like I was carrying around this humongous load and I needed to exhale.

"I owe you so much and I'll always be here for you, please know that. Now tell me what's on your mind."

"The charges are all true." Blair almost dropped her champagne glass when the words left my mouth.

"Diamond, I'm not gonna lie, that was the last thing I expected you to tell me. How...when...I have so many questions."

"Let's go sit down at our table and I'll give you the full story."

Blair sat speechless for about an hour as I took her on my journey from disgruntled baby mama to a ballin' bitch."

"So all that talk about investments were what..."

"Girl, the only thing I was investing in was that coke."

"Wow! I'm stunned. I can't believe I..."

"Sorry to cut you off but I've been waiting for this call. Hold up," I said before answering. "Hello."

"Meet me at my spot in Edgewater at 5. Don't be late."

"I won't."

"Who was that?" Blair questioned when the

call ended.

"My last hope."

"Huh?" Blair was clearly perplexed by my statement.

"Lets just say if the person I just got off the phone with can't get me out of this fucked up predicament then those twenty-five years might become my reality."

"Does Cameron know?"

"Hell No! Only you and it's going to stay like that."

"Diamond, my lips are sealed. I put that on everything but Cameron has a lot of resources he might be able to help you is all I'm saying."

"He's already paying my legal fees and that's enough. Plus, I want Cameron to keep his hands clean. In case anything goes wrong I don't want him caught up in the middle of it. He has way too much to lose. Right now he believes I'm innocent and to the media he is simply supporting his girlfriend. I can't make him an accessory after the fact."

"I hear you, but girl you got me worried," Blair admitted.

"So am I, but honestly finally having somebody to talk openly about it with, has relieved me of some of my stress. So thanks for listening."

"I wish I could do more. You always come through for me, I'm never able to return the favor."

"Blair, just being here as my friend is a blessing in itself. I've wanted to purge my soul but had nobody to do so with."

"Listen, I don't care where I am or what time of the day or night it is you can always call on me."

"Thank you and I love you for that," I said giving her a hug. "I hate to cut this short but I have to go. I'm not sure how that traffic is going to be going into Jersey and I can't be late."

"No, go 'head. I totally understand but make sure you call me later and let me know you're good."

"Will do." I hugged Blair one more time and made my exit.

Kennedy

As I was wrapping up a call with a magazine that was considering doing a feature on Blair, I noticed my cell was ringing. "Marcus, hello," I said right on cue, as I hung up the landline phone without missing the cell call.

"How's everything going with you, Kennedy?"

"Good but I'm hoping they're about to get even better," I smiled, leaning back in my chair.

"Remember I said I would call you when I thought I had a part for Blair."

"Of course I remember." I sat straight up in my chair gripping the phone tighter.

"There is a role I think she'll be perfect for but of course I need her to come to LA and audition."

"When?"

"The end of next week. Are you both available? Because I would also like to meet with you and discuss the PR situation with Lionsgate."

"We certainly will be available. Just send me over all the necessary information."

"Will do."

"Marcus, before you go, can you give me a few details about the part?"

"It's a supporting role but a very important one. She'll be playing a woman who is in Grad school but is also the mistress of the President of the United States that eventually ends up dead."

"What point in the movie does she die?"

"The middle. "

"It sounds juicy!"

"It is. Whatever young lady lands this part will be the next big thing in Hollywood."

"Who is playing the President?"

"Denzel Washington just signed on."

"Unbelievable!"

"I told you it was huge. But when I read the role of Liza, that's the character's name in the movie, I immediately thought of Blair."

"Marcus, thank you so much."

"You know I'm a man of my word."

"Yes you are. I'll wait for your email and I'll speak to you soon."

I literally jumped out my chair when I hung up with Marcus. "Yes..Yes...Yes!!!!!" I screamed pumping my fist in the air. The way I was carrying on you would've thought Blair already got the part but in my gut she had, and at the moment that's all that mattered.

Luckily it was past office hours and everybody was gone because if Darcy had seen me celebrating she would've shut that shit down. But nothing was getting me off the emotional high I was on. As I made my way to the elevator I called Blair to share the news but her phone went straight to voicemail.

"Hey Blair! It's me Kennedy. Call me as soon as you get this message. I have some exciting news?" I decided to wait and give her the specifics when she called me back, so we could scream in excitement together.

"Blair I told you I would take you to the top," I said out loud talking to myself full of enthusiasm as the elevator doors opened. I almost coughed when I saw a familiar face step out. "Darcy already left for the day," I said about to get on the elevator.

"No, I'm here for you."

"For me...why?"

"Let's not play games, Kennedy. I'm aware that Blair is staying with you."

"And?"

"I have a problem with that."

"Then I suggest you discuss that with Blair. I have no interest in getting involved with her personal life, Michael."

"If that was the case you wouldn't have let her move in with you."

"We're friends, of course she can stay with me."

"You're a lot more than friends."

"Excuse me?"

"How do you think Darcy will feel when she

finds out you've been running your own PR business behind her back?"

"I don't know what the hell you're talking about!"

"Save the denials for your boss although I'm sure she won't believe any of it. As you know, Kennedy I'm a very powerful man in this city and I can find out pretty much anything that I want. I know it was you that got Blair the feature in Skee Patron video. You've been getting her all this media coverage by telling people that she is one of Darcy's clients. When we both know that's a lie."

"What do you want, Michael?"

"I want you to stop selling Blair a dream that she is going to be some big star when being in a Skee Patron video is the best she'll ever get."

"Oh, I get it now. You've fooled Blair into believing that you're this confident, successful man and she's not good enough for you. But you're really an insecure prick who's afraid that if Blair finds her own success, she'll realize that she doesn't need you."

"I think you need to watch your mouth and be very careful."

"Mr. Michael Frost," I made sure to say his name with extreme sarcasm. "Men like you don't intimidate me. I will keep representing Blair and not only that I will take her to the top. Now excuse me, I have things to do for my client," I snapped and brushed past him. When I got on the elevator I quickly hit the close button because I had no desire to ride down with him. Michael was good at playing the in control lawyer type, but I sensed he had a darkness looming within him so I didn't want him in my space.

A few moments after I stepped off the elevator my cell started ringing and it was Blair. "Hey, Girl!"

"Hey! I just got your message. What's so urgent?"

"You remember Marcus from Lionsgate?"

"Of course!"

"Well, he called me today and there is a part he wants you to audition for."

"Stop lying! Are you serious?"

"Yes! You would play Denzel Washington's mistress and he is the President Of The United States. So no you're not Michelle but Denzel certainly is a great second option to Obama."

"Did you say Denzel Washington...I would be in a movie with like the best actor in Hollywood right now! This can't be my life."

"Yes it is and it's only going to get better. I promise!"

"So what do I have to do to get this part?"

"Next week we're going to LA so you can audition. Are you ready for that?"

"Hell yeah! I'm nervous but I'm ready. This is the type of opportunity I've been waiting for and because of you I have it. Thank you so much, Kennedy!"

"I'm just doing my job."

"You're doing a lot more than just your job and please know I'm so grateful."

"Thank you. I've seen you evolve in such a short span of time and I'm so proud of you. I think you're going all the way and I'll be right there cheering you on."

"You're wonderful for my self esteem...thank you," she laughed. "I hate to rush you off the phone but I have to call Diamond. She is going to lose it!"

"You do that and I'll see you later on." When I hung up with Blair I was glad that I went with my first instinct and didn't tell her about my confrontation with Michael. I wanted her to enjoy her moment and not have it ruined by an asshole like Michael. When I got home I would tell her and hopefully we would both have a good laugh about it.

Blair

On my way back to Kennedy's apartment I kept trying to call Diamond, but I wasn't getting an answer. I knew she went to Jersey after we had lunch earlier but I figured she would've been done by now. I tried to dial Diamond's number one more time as I was getting the key out of my purse to open the front door to the building Kennedy lived in. Diamond once again didn't answer but right when I was about to leave a message I felt somebody walk up behind me.

"How does it feel going from a doorman building to a measly walkup?" I instantly recognized the arrogant voice.

"Michael, what are you doing here?" I asked, turning around to face him.

"I would think you'd already know the answer to that. And you still didn't answer my question."

"What question?"

"How does it feel going from living in a luxury doorman building to this?" he stated crudely as he lifted his left hand and pointed towards the modest building.

"You know, I'm in a great mood and I refuse to let you and your negativity ruin it."

"I had no idea that being in some hip hop video would do that for you. You feel proud being some video girl. I thought I taught you better than that."

"For your information I am proud of the video I did with Skee Patron and that's just the beginning. That career I always wanted and you never supported is gonna happen for me."

"I hope you're not counting on your friend Kennedy to make that happen for you because pretty soon she won't even be able to pay her rent, let alone help you with a career."

"What do you mean by that?"

"I'm assuming she didn't tell you about our conversation today."

"As a matter of fact she did," I lied, not wanting Michael to feel like once again he had the upper hand.

"Then you're aware that as soon as I tell Darcy that Kennedy has been representing you under false pretenses that she'll be fired. Since I know you don't have any money that's going to leave her pretty much fucked."

"Why would you do something like that? Kennedy has never done anything to you!"

"I made her a fair offer and she refused so now she has to pay the consequences. I'm going to make you an offer too and I advise you to weigh your options carefully. You can continue to follow this going nowhere dream of being a famous actress or you can come back to me while the door is still open, because if you make me wait too long and I decide to close that door on you, you'll have nothing. So again, I advise you to weigh your options carefully and make the decision that's in your best interest."

Michael turned and walked away leaving me in turmoil. I ran upstairs to Kennedy's apartment and threw my purse down before falling back on the couch. I stared up at the ceiling replaying every word Michael said to me. By the third replay I heard Kennedy opening the front door.

"Hey, Superstar!" she beamed, standing in the living room.

"Hey," I responded in a low unenthusiastic tone.

"What the hell is wrong with you? What happened to that bubbly voice that was on the other end of my phone like an hour or so ago?"

"Michael happened...that's what."

"Gosh, I was hoping he stayed away from you at least one day so you could enjoy the good news," Kennedy huffed, as she slumped over in the chair across from me.

"I wish you would've told me. I tried my best not to let Michael know that he had gotten to me but

I don't know how convincing I was."

"Fuck Michael! You'll be fine without him."

"So you're not worried about losing your job?"

"That's what that asshole told you?" Kennedy sat up and glared at me.

"Yeah he did. I had no idea Darcy didn't know you were getting gigs for me. I will admit I was wondering why she didn't have you drop me, after our confrontation and she found out we were sleeping with the same man but I figured she chose business over a man...how dumb am I."

"Listen, I've been wanting to give Darcy the middle finger for a while now but Diamond came up with one of her great ideas and it sounded good at the time. But I have no regrets. Plus, I know Diamond is going to beat those charges and we'll be able to open up our own PR Company like we planned on doing."

"I don't know if Diamond will be able to do that anytime soon."

"Why would you say that...did she tell you something?" Kennedy sounded distraught and her eyes widened with a look of fear.

"No! It's nothing like that," I said, trying to reassure her. "I just know with court cases they can be draining you know..." I hated lying to Kennedy, but Diamond was my best friend and I promised her I wouldn't say anything. But if Kennedy was counting on this new business venture with Diamond to save the day I was scared for both of us.

"Girl, you had me shook for a sec! I thought you had some inside scoop I wasn't aware of. Thank goodness you don't! I feel much better about dealing with Darcy tomorrow. Basically I can tell that Bitch to kiss my ass if she decides she wants to fire me or better yet I might just quit and not even give her the chance."

"Kennedy, you know I have zero love for Darcy but first see what she has to say before you think about quitting. Michael could just be spitting bullshit and have no intention of telling Darcy anything."

"True, but honestly I don't care at this point. I'm tired of dealing with Darcy's bullshit."

"I get that but you always tell me to think smart."

"Look at you being the mature one in the situation and giving me advice," Kennedy smiled and playfully smacked my knee. "I'll follow your advice. If Darcy plays nice then I won't quit. I'll deal with her bullshit a tad bit longer so Diamond can resolve her situation. But I can't wait to give that demon the deuces."

"Enough about Darcy and Michael lets talk about my audition in LA next week. I still can't believe this is really happening for me."

"Believe it! I knew Marcus was impressed with you and would come through but I didn't think it would be this soon and such an incredible role."

"Now all I have to do is get the part."

"You will! And I'm going to keep working the media so more and more people can keep seeing your face and trust me more opportunities will present themselves."

"I can't believe the buzz being in that Skee Patron video has gotten me. That shit is crazy."

"Oh fuck! How could I forget?"

"Forget what?"

"Skee Patron's publicist hit me up today. Between Marcus calling me, getting threatened by Michael," she laughed rolling her eyes, "and then coming home and finding you in a slump I forgot I got some work for you. Nothing major, but beneficial all the same."

"Spill it."

"Skee is hosting a party at this spot called Beauty and Essex tomorrow night. They're paying him a grip but he wants you to attend with him and you'll also get paid."

"Huh...whose idea was that?"

"Not sure but I know his publicist was intrigued by those photos I had go out to all the media outlets with you on that dinner date with Kirk. That's why I was able to convince them to give you a nice fee. And we'll get plenty of press from this."

"Your schemes always seem to work out in my favor."

"I must admit I did learn a few tricks from

watching Darcy in action. What's so great is that I get to utilize them on you."

'This is incredible! I'm about to get paid to party. I would've never thought."

"Trust me, there is more of that to come. If I keep circulating the right photos of you with the right people and get you a couple of magazine features I'll be able to get you a ton of paying hosting gigs but we want you to be selective. You just can't host any gig. That way when you do host a party it will seem exclusive so you can ask for that exclusive money... you feel me?"

"No doubt and as always your strategy is on point."

"I try...I try..." Kennedy smiled and I couldn't help but smile right along with her.

Diamond

When I pulled up to Renny's townhouse that almost seemed secretly located on the riverfront in Edgewater, New Jersey, I took a deep breath before getting out the car. Not only had he been my drug connect for the past couple years he was also the man I was placing my future on.

Renaldo 'Renny' ONeal went from dominating the borough of Queens to taking over major markets on the East Coast on the low. After the murder of his cousin Arnez and nonstop street drugs wars he decided to keep a low profile. Most dealers didn't even know the majority of their product came courtesy of Renny. Not only did he have some of the best products and prices he had the right connections to get my situation handled. It was just a matter if he would do it or not.

"Thanks for seeing me," I said to Renny when he opened the door.

"You've been a client of mine for a while, I

figured I could at least hear what you have to say."

"You know I wouldn't come to you unless it was important, especially under the circumstances."

"Yeah, and your circumstances aren't looking too good."

"You're right and that's why I need you."

"Diamond, you know I'm not one that likes to listen to a lot of bullshit so tell me what you need." I swallowed hard before I answered Renny's question. I was scared because if he said no, I would literally feel like my life was over and I wasn't ready to become hopeless.

"My lawyer said my indictment is currently sealed. I believe I know who their informant is but I need you to find out for sure and have whoever is set to testify against me taken care of. But of course it has to be done in a way that doesn't connect back to me."

"That is some request," Renny responded, pouring himself a drink. "You believe if this is taken care of all your legal issues will disappear?"

"Yes I do. I'm positive."

"You do realize now that you're on the State's watch list it never stops. They'll always be waiting for the right moment to get you again, even if I'm able to make all this disappear."

"Well they won't have anything to get because I'm out of the game." Renny raised his eyebrow, clearly surprised by my statement.

"So you're done with the drug business?" his tone made it clear he wasn't convinced.

"Yes. I was planning on easing my way out this business before any of this went down."

"Why is that? It's been lucrative for you."

"After I was robbed I started having some reservations."

"Well that was your fault. I told you a long time ago you needed to lay your head in a much more secure location."

"You're right."

"But you're over in that fancy high rise now, what's the problem?"

"That's the other thing. Cameron has been so good to me and my daughter and..."

"You talking about that basketball player," he said cutting me off.

"Yes, and even with all this drug and attempted murder charges looming over me he's had my back."

"Have you admitted to him that the charges are true?"

"Hell No! I would never want him to know about that part of my life. I want to get my life together so I can be a girlfriend he can be proud of."

"I hear you. So you get out of the drug game, then what's next?"

"I've made a lot of money and I have a nice stash. I wanted to use a large part of that money to start a public relations company with a friend of mine. She's already in that business and has a lot of relationships. I believe we can be very successful with it."

"I still remember when I first met you. You was fuckin' around wit' that no good nigga, just had your daughter and wanted a way to support the two of you. When you finally did start making some money you stood by your word and cut that nigga off. I could respect that. And I can also respect you wanting to get out the game."

"Does that mean you'll help me?"

"Yes it does and the reason why is because ever since I've known you, you've always tried to help yourself."

"Renny, I can't even put into words how grateful I am."

"I know that you are. But understand something, Diamond." Renny paused for a few moments as if making sure he had my full attention and I was listening carefully. "This favor comes at a very high price and when I collect I expect you to deliver...no questions asked."

I knew that price Renny was talking about had nothing to do with money. He was basically putting it on the table that if he came through for me I owed him my fuckin' life literally. But my back was so far pushed against the wall I would've taken a deal with the devil to stay out of jail and be able to raise my daughter.

"You have my word. If you make this go away I'll be forever indebted to you. So whenever it's time for you to collect I'll be ready."

"I'm glad we're on the same page."

"We are." I wanted to assure him.

"I won't be in contact with you to let you know when this is done. More than likely you'll hear about it from your lawyer. And there is no need for you to call and thank me afterwards...are we clear?"

"A hundred percent. I'm not gonna take up any more of your time, but before I go I want to tell you now...thank you." Renny simply nodded his head acknowledging my appreciation. "By the way how is your wife?"

"Nichelle is good. Her modeling agency is doing quite well. If you follow through with your public relations company I will definitely make sure she sends some business your way."

"Thank you so much, Renny. You really are too good to me."

"Take care, Diamond."

When I left Renny's crib I thought a sense of relief would come over me but instead I felt a type of anxiety. I think it was because now I was about to play the waiting game. Renny gave me no exact time when he would handle the problem so no doubt I would be driving myself crazy wondering when he pressed the go button. But again, my hands were tied and I had no choice but to deal with it.

"Babe, you finally home. I was calling you and you didn't answer your phone," Cameron said, when I walked through the door.

"Sorry about that. I left my phone at the restaurant I had lunch at with Blair earlier today. Then by the time I got it back it had died and I don't know what happened to my car charger," I lied. "The first thing I'm going to do is put this bad boy on a charger. I'm sure I missed a ton of calls," I continued, before rushing into my bedroom and doing exactly that so my story seemed believable. I couldn't tell Cameron the truth. That I was begging my drug connect to murder whoever might be an informant in my criminal case.

"You left your phone and you got it back...how lucky are you," I heard him say from my bedroom.

"Yeah, we had a good waitress," I smiled, coming back into the living room giving Cameron a kiss. "I missed you today."

"How much?"

"This much," I said, before sliding my tongue down his throat.

"I like that," Cameron murmured between kisses. " I missed you too and I'm about to show you just how much."

"Is that right?" I questioned in a flirtatious

tone.

"Yep, but only if you want me to."

"You don't even have to ask," I said taking Cameron's hand and leading him into my bedroom. By the time we reached my bed we were both practically undressed. Cameron wasted no time gliding his massive tool inside of me as if he knew how wet my pussy was. "Damn, baby, I needed this," I confessed.

"So did I," he moaned, as each stroke seemed to relieve me of all my anxiety. I had no idea sex was such a stress reliever. I arched my back as he went deeper and deeper inside of me. As his tongue massaged my nipples he then began sprinkling my stomach with kisses. My body began this buildup sensation but then when Cameron slid his dick out and replaced it with his unbelievable tongue magic I couldn't hold back any longer. I pressed my nails into his flesh as he continued to tongue fuck my clit.

Right when I thought my pleasure had reached it's limit, Cameron then glided his dick back inside of me. His strokes became more powerful, meaningful and intense as we both were about to reach our climax. I cried out in pure ecstasy as he exploded inside of me.

"I love you, Cameron."

"I love you too," he said, as we both began to drift off to sleep. Lying in Cameron's arms seemed to restore me. Like he was transferring all his strength over to me. Being with him gave me everything I needed to forget about my troubles and get lost in love. Right when I was about to go into a meditative state, the non-stop ringing of my cell wouldn't allow that to happen. I tried to ignore it and got pissed with myself for not putting it on vibrate. Finally I decided to answer because not only did I want to fall asleep I didn't want the constant ringing to wake Cameron up.

"Hello." I answered in a low somewhat groggy voice. At first the person on the other end didn't say anything so I said hello again. Right when I was about to hang up the person finally spoke up.

"I don't know what the fuck you thought but you ain't gonna get away wit' shit. You a dead bitch. Bye bye, baby." I wanted to scream out to the unrecognizable male voice but they hung up. When I looked at the caller ID it was an unknown number. I rested my head back in Cameron's protective arms, but I closed my eyes with the words you a dead bitch replaying in my mind.

Kennedy

I decided to stride into work looking extra cute and extra confident. If Darcy did decide to bring the bullshit I wanted to make sure I at least appeared like I didn't give two fucks. Within five minutes sitting at my desk I was glad I did because Darcy called me into her office. Before I went I pulled out the compact mirror from my purse and applied extra lip-gloss. I wanted my lips to be extra poppin' if our conversation led to a war of words.

"Good morning, Darcy, what can I do for you?"

"Besides get down on your knees and beg for your job, not too much."

"I always gotta kick out of your sense of humor."

"This isn't a joke and you definitely shouldn't be taking what I'm saying lightly. Michael informed me about what you've been doing. How dare you use the company I built and the brand I created to promote some lowlife whore!"

"Wouldn't you be the whore in this scenario since Michael was technically Blair's man."

"How dare you! Michael is with me and whatever he had going on with that thing meant nothing. She's irrelevant to him."

"If Blair is so irrelevant, why did Michael come to this office last night trying to get me to stop representing her? Huh?"

"Because, he was looking out for my best interest! He didn't appreciate you taking advantage of me."

"Clearly those tracks are sewed too tight in your head because you sound absolutely delusional. The only person taking advantage of your stupidity is Michael."

"Before you take this too far and say something you can't take back I'm going to give you one option. Relinquish all representation of Blair, effective immediately."

"Now why would I do that?"

"Because you love your job and are grateful to have one. Need I say more?"

"You're right, I do love my job but I hate working for your unappreciative ass. You work me like a slave, never give me the commission I'm entitled to and my paycheck barely covers my rent. If you think I'm going to beg you to keep this job then you can kick rocks. As a matter of fact you can take this job and shove it up your bony ass."

"You're willing to risk your entire career over that going nowhere bimbo! You're a bigger fool than I thought!"

"No, what made me the fool was putting up with your bullshit for all this time. But while you're throwing around the term fool, you should apply it to yourself. You're about to have a hernia over a man that isn't thinking about you."

"You're going to regret siding with that zero and losing your job. Once I'm done with you, you won't be able to get another job in this business anywhere!" Darcy's face was on fire when she made the threat.

"So you say. I think you give yourself way too much credit. Not only am I giving you and your company deuces, I promise you that Blair's light will only get brighter and she will be a star."

"Get the hell out of my office and clear out your desk! And you better not ever set foot in this building again," Darcy warned.

"That's one thing you'll never have to worry about. But so you know just because you fired me, it's not going to make Michael want you or respect you. He's using you because he doesn't want Blair to have any success. But you're so pathetic and desperate for a man, you're playing right into his hand. But good luck with that because you're truly my motivation to make sure Blair wins."

I strolled out of Darcy's office with a huge smile

on my face. It felt so damn good to tell that witch to basically fuck off. I was so hyped that I finally got to serve her ass that I wasn't yet concerned over the fact that I was now unemployed.

"Kennedy, what happened in there? When I came in the office all I heard was yelling but I couldn't understand what was being said," Tammy said, with an expression full of curiosity.

"I was fired or maybe I quit...who knows but one thing that's a fact is I no longer work here," I grinned as I started gathering all of my personal items off my desk.

"Darcy fired you! But you basically run this business for her, why would she do that?"

"Dick!"

Tammy accidentally spit out the water she was drinking after I said that. "Girl, you did not say dick!" she repeated, now laughing.

"Yes the hell I did and it's true. Darcy is so thirsty to score brownie points with Michael that she threw me all the way under the bus."

"Michael...oh Michael the guy her and Blair were both seeing."

"Yes. He came here last night and demanded I stop doing PR for Blair or he would tell Darcy that I was basically running my own business behind her back and he stayed true to his threat."

"Wow! As pissed as Darcy is now, when her anger subsides she's going to regret getting rid of you."

"Maybe she will maybe she won't but I don't care either way. I've been miserable working for her far too long."

"So what are you going to do now?"

"You know Michael did me a favor by outing me to Darcy because now I can focus on doing my own thing."

"So are you going to start your own company?"

"That's the plan!"

"No wonder you don't seem to be stressing about what happened. Do you think I can come work for you? You're the only reason I look forward to showing up."

"I appreciate that, I really do. I tell you what. Once I get my situation right they'll be a job waiting for you."

"Are you serious?"

"Yes! You've been working here for free but bust yo' ass like you raking in a six-figure salary. I need people like you but of course I'll make sure you not only get your college credits but you'll also get a paycheck."

"Thank you! I hope it works out for you soon."

"So do I. But until it does hold things down here..."

"That won't be necessary because Tammy you're fired too," Darcy said walking up from behind and cutting me off.

"But I didn't do anything."

"You're guilty by association. Now pack up your stuff too. You can both get out."

"But I need my credits for school."

"Not my problem."

"Please don't do this. Can I at least finish out my semester," Tammy pleaded.

"Nope. And if you don't hurry I'm going to have security escort you out. So get your shit and go."

"Darcy, you are below scum, if there's such a thing. And, Tammy, don't worry you'll find another internship. Now lets get out of here before they have to call an ambulance to pick her," I nodded my head towards Darcy, "off the floor." As we walked out I heard Darcy rambling on but didn't pay attention to any of her words. I was closing the chapter on her and focusing on my future.

When I arrived on Thompson St. in Soho to meet Diamond and Blair for lunch I was awe-struck at the décor in the restaurant. As I made my way to the table the two of them were already seated at. I entered a sunken living room that had a centerpiece of traditional crystal chandeliers. The chandeliers were classic and elegant which created a sense of a royal banquet hall. Then the surrounding balcony dinning rooms featured contemporary wall decorations and a montage of mirrors.

"Yo, this place is beautiful," I said to Diamond and Blair when I finally took my seat.

"That's what I said to Blair when I got here."

"So, Blair you picked this spot?"

"Yeah, Michael took me here a few times and I loved it. I could never afford to go on my own but I got my check today for doing that Skee Patron video so I thought we could celebrate on me!"

"I'm so happy for you, Blair! I love to see you making your own money and smiling about it."

"I appreciate that, Diamond but I owe it to you and Kennedy. The both of you believed in me way more than I believed in myself and I thank both of you."

"Well, this is just one check of many more to come. Did you tell Diamond about the audition in LA coming up for the movie role?"

"She sure did and I am ecstatic! If I didn't have this court bullshit looming over my head I would go to LA with you guys."

"How is that court stuff coming?" I inquired, hoping Diamond would have some good news.

"It's coming along. I'm feeling optimistic that things will work out in my favor. I still need some time to get things together but I feel good."

"Glad to hear that because now that I'm unemployed I need this business of ours to jump off."

"What do you mean you're unemployed?"

"Fuck! What she means is Michael followed through on his threat."

"Hold up! The two of you are confusing me. What threat and what does Michael have to do with this?"

"He came to see Kennedy last night at her job and told her that if she didn't stop representing me that he would tell Darcy she was doing business behind her back."

"Are you serious!"

"Yep, and when I got to work this morning sure enough Darcy called me into her office and made the same threat and on top of that she said I had to beg to keep my job. The two of them are truly made for each other. They are both controlling assholes."

"Kennedy, I feel horrible about this. I was hoping Michael was bluffing."

"I feel bad because I'm the one who gave Kennedy the idea to start running her own business but using Darcy's resources while doing so."

"Neither one of you should feel bad, the woman is a monster. She even got rid of Tammy."

"The intern?"

"Yes! And she said she was going to drag my name through the mud so I couldn't get another job in this industry."

"All of that because you were doing some

other business on the side?" Diamond asked.

"No, it's because of her jealously towards Blair. She was still willing to let me keep my job but wanted me to agree to stop doing PR for Blair. I told her she was pathetic."

"You did!" both Blair and Diamond looked at me with surprise.

"Yes, it's the truth and she needed to know. Michael used her to try and punish you," I pointed towards Blair, "but her jealously wouldn't let her see it. She played right into his hands. But I guess because I'm not hypnotized by the dick like she is she can't see it."

"I still feel bad, Kennedy. Now you have no job and besides this hosting gig tonight with Skee I don't have any money coming in. We're fucked," Blair sighed, leaning her head to the side.

"No you guys aren't fucked. Kennedy will continue doing what she does best which is creating stars and Blair you're going to be that star."

"That's going to be kind of hard for her to do without a job."

"She does have a job."

"I do?" I questioned, not following what Diamond was saying.

"Yes, you're going to go 'head and move on that business offer I proposed to you."

"But you just said you needed more time."

"I need some time but that doesn't have

anything to do with you. I can still fund the company but until I get my situation resolved I wouldn't be on any of the paperwork. You can think of me as your silent partner."

"Diamond, you are beyond a sweetheart. I know you're only doing this to help me."

"I want to help you and Blair. Both of you have come so far and just because I'm dealing with some bullshit right now, don't mean all the progress you've made has to stop."

"You're amazing. I feel so honored to have you as a best friend," Blair said as her eyes started to water up.

"You are not about to start crying...waitress come here please. We're going to need a bottle of your best champagne. We have some celebrating to do! And ladies, don't worry it's on me," Diamond winked.

Blair

"Fuck! I can't decide which outfit to wear," I yelled out loud while staring at myself in the full-length mirror. "Kennedy, come here please," I called out, needing a second opinion.

"What you in here yelling about?"

"Clothes! Your stylist friend Rebecca dropped off two outfits for me to choose from to wear tonight. But I can't decide between the cutout mini or the flowing chiffon dress.

"That one is breathtaking and the teal blue is gorgeous," Kennedy said, pointing to the chiffon dress with the plunging neckline. "But it's more red carpet Emmy ready then sexy host for club party attire. So go with the mini and the sparkly silver color will really pop on pictures."

"I totally agree but I just love this Alexandre Vauthier dress."

"So do I but trust me you'll have another opportunity to wear it."

"Yeah, I need to hold onto this one."

"Who's going to do your makeup? That definitely has to be on point, because I'm going to work the hell out of these pictures you take."

"Cornelius should be here shortly to make this face camera ready. I'ma go hop in the shower and get dressed. Listen out for him in case I'm still in the bathroom when he gets here."

"Got you. But he's going to have to do you up quick because Skee will be picking you up shortly."

"I thought a car service was coming to get me."

"Yeah it is but Skee will be in the car too...what you thought you were meeting him there?"

"Yes, I did."

"What would be the point of you all appearing as a couple if you didn't show up together, wouldn't that defeat the purpose."

"I suppose but I didn't realize we were trying to give the impression we were a couple."

"Were you not listening to anything I said when I brought this to you?"

"No, I think I got stuck on the part about being paid to do this. Getting a check was the only thing on my mind."

"Then all you have to do is go with the flow tonight and you'll walk away with a very nice payment before you leave."

"So I'll get the money tonight?"

"Yes!"

"You're right I need to hurry up! We both know I can't afford to miss out on making some money!" I heard Kennedy laughing at my comment while walking off.

I rushed in the shower, got dressed and makeup/hair done in record time. "How do I look?" I stood up and asked Kennedy when Cornelius finished.

"Sickening, Bitch!" Cornelius exclaimed, snapping his fingers before Kennedy even had a chance to respond.

"I have to agree with Cornelius, you look incredibly amazing! Skee and this team will be super impressed. When the paparazzi see the two of you step out they are going to go crazy."

"I hope you're right."

"Trust me I am and hopefully I can line you up some even bigger paying gigs. So make sure when you step out the car your swag walk is on point and you give just the right smile to the cameras. Got it?"

"Got it."

"Now get your purse and get downstairs. Tish just sent me a text saying Skee is waiting for you."

"See you guys later and wish me luck," I said, waving goodbye.

While making my way down the stairs trying not to bust my ass in the six-inch heels I was wearing I realized Kirk was calling me. At first I wasn't going to answer but we were becoming extremely close in the last few weeks and I didn't want to mess that up. "Hey, Kirk!"

"What's up gorgeous. I know it's last minute but I wanted you to go to this party with me at Beauty and Essex tonight."

"I would but I'm already going with Skee. And before you jump to any conclusions it's strictly business. I'm getting paid to show up with him."

"I'm disappointed but I understand. How about dinner tomorrow?"

"Would love to."

"Cool. I know you on a date tonight but don't act like you can't speak when you see me tonight."

We both laughed before I said, "I won't and I can't wait for our *real* date tomorrow. Bye."

When I got outside I saw a black four door Bentley parked out front and knew that had to be my ride. As I got closer the driver stepped out so he could open the door for me. Skee and a female were in the car and I assumed the woman was his publicist Tish. Both of their eyes showed approval when they looked at me before I got in.

"Damn, you gon' make a nigga put you on my permanent payroll looking like that," Skee said, not cracking a smile.

"I see you haven't lost your sense of humor."

"Two things I don't joke about are compliments and my money. Honestly, you look beautiful tonight but you got eyes. You already knew that when you walked out the door. I feel proud to have you on my arm tonight."

"And I feel proud to be on your arm," I smiled, crossing my leg to highlight the mind-blowing shoes I had on. I felt like cinde-fuckin-rella.

When the chauffer driven Bentley stopped in front of the venue there was a line down the block and paparazzi taking pics of other celebrities as they walked the red carpet. All that came to a halt when the driver opened the door and Skee and I stepped out holding hands. Not only did the photographers turn all cameras on us people in line pulled out their phones and began snapping away. I thought about the advice Kennedy gave me before I left and instantly turned up my swag as we made our way inside the club.

A waitress and several security men were waiting at the entrance to escort us to our booth in VIP. Bottles were already on ice and Skee's new song that featured me in his video was blaring out the sound system. Skee didn't let go of my hand until we reached our seats and for a moment I really started thinking we were a couple. Even after we sat down he was so attentive like a real boyfriend. He made sure my glass of champagne was poured first and kept asking me did I need anything. Our night started off perfectly.

"Skee, I need the two of you to take some pictures for the photographer," I heard Tish tell Skee. After her request, Skee took my hand and I tried to give my best top model poses. As the camera flashed I noticed Kirk and a few of his NBA teammates get seated at a booth across from ours. I kept posing, reminding myself I was on a paid job working. For our last pic, Skee caught me off guard by kissing me on the lips but I played along with it and kissed him back. I wasn't sure if it was because of the three glasses of champagne I already had but I had to admit, I actually enjoyed it too.

A few minutes after taking our last picture and we sat back down, Kirk walked over to our booth. "What's up, Skee and how you doing, Blair?"

"I'm good. How are you?" I said standing up giving Kirk a hug and a kiss on his cheek. Instantly the cameras started snapping and I wasn't expecting that although I should've known since I had arrived with the biggest rap star and I was now hugging one of the biggest NBA stars.

"Better now after that hug. Every time I see you, you look more beautiful than the last time."

"Don't make me blush."

"I won't and I'm not gonna hold you up. I just wanted to speak and tell you how great you look tonight."

"Thank you," I smiled.

"You welcome and I'll see you tomorrow night."

"I see the two of you are still close," Skee commented when I sat down.

"Yeah, we are."

"I hope you being here with me isn't going to cause you any problems with him," Skee said, handing me another glass of champagne.

"No, he understands."

"That's good. So are you enjoying yourself?"

"Of course! This is my first time doing this club thing like this. The DJ has shouted out my name like three times already. They're making me feel like I'm some sort of a celebrity."

"You are and it's only going to get better." Skee then nodded his head at the security team that was standing beside him and they then stood around our booth creating a man made wall. It shielded us from everybody else in the club. I didn't know what was going on. "Here take this," he said handing me a clear capsule that had a whitish flaky powder inside of it.

"What's this?"

"A Molly. You've never had one?"

"No."

"Aren't you the innocent one. This is nice you can try it for the first time with me." Skee then put a capsule in his mouth and washed it down with a bottle of water. At first I was hesitant to take the pill but I again thought back to what Kennedy said about going with the flow so I followed Skee's lead.

"Is this going to make me feel funny?"

"That depends on your definition of funny," he laughed. "Lets just say you're about to be in love with love," Skee said, laughing some more. I didn't understand what he meant until about thirty minutes later. It was like a big dose of serotonin was released in my body at once and I was overcome with happiness. It was like all my senses were heightened from the sound of the music to the touch of Skee's hand on my thigh.

I reached for another glass of champagne but Skee stopped me. "Have some more water instead," he insisted. "I don't want you to get dehydrated."

"Okay, but can I have another Molly?"

"Of course," he smiled, willingly handing it over to me. After an hour or so I decided that a Molly gave me the most unbelievable feeling in the world. I had never experienced anything like it. I felt alive and free. I stood up and started moving to the music. All of my inhibitions were gone. Skee then started moving to the music with me. He had his hands on my waist and we started kissing. But this wasn't like our first kiss, brief and harmless. This kiss was passionate with our tongues seducing each other.

The kiss was intense as if I was falling in love with Skee. Although I knew that couldn't be true I still embraced the feeling of it being so. The high had us caught up in each other like no one else in the club existed, that was until Tish came and interrupted us.

"Skee, that's enough. Everybody is watching the two of you and taking pictures," she tried to say loud enough that he could hear her but low enough that nobody else would. When I turned around, I realized she was right. The security was no longer our wall. They had moved back to the side after we took the pills so our tongue session was on public display. The damage it might have caused didn't hit until I locked eyes with Kirk. He didn't take his eyes off of me and before I knew it he was standing directly in front of my face.

"I thought this was strictly business. What part of business is putting your tongue down this nigga's throat?" I stood there at a loss of words.

"Is there a problem?" Skee stepped in and asked.

"Nah, ain't no problem. She's all yours."

"I know she is. Aren't I a lucky man," Skee stated to Kirk as they stared each other down. I saw Kirk's jaw clench and he balled up his fist. The security noticed it too because they quickly came forward letting both men know they didn't want a problem. Kirk gave me the look of death and stormed off.

"Do you want another one," Skee whispered in my ear and I nodded yes. And just like that I decided to forget my encounter with Kirk because I wanted to get back to enjoying my high.

When we finally decided to leave the club, we walked out holding hands and I was feeling better than ever. Once we got inside the Bentley we started back up kissing. Luckily Skee had one of his security men take Tish home so we had the entire backseat to ourselves. We couldn't keep our hands off each other.

"I want you to come home with me," Skee whispered in my ear.

"I want that too," I whispered back.

"Take us to my place," Skee informed the driver as we both sat up, choosing to put a pause on our make out session until we were behind closed doors, although we continued to hold hands. Right when I started to get comfortable my cell started ringing. I decided to ignore it but it wouldn't stop.

"I think you should answer it," Skee suggested after it kept ringing back to back. When I unzipped my purse and look to see who was phone stalking me I realized it was Kennedy.

"Hey, is everything okay?" I questioned when I heard what sounded like sobbing on the other end of the phone. "Kennedy, what's wrong?" It took her a few minutes to respond and in the midst of that I started getting a migraine and losing my high from anticipation.

"No, everything is not okay," Kennedy finally said between sobs.

"What is it? You're scaring me!"

"It's Diamond."

"What about Diamond?"

"She's Dead." After Kennedy said those words the last thing I remembered was dropping the phone and everything going black.

Baller Bitches Volume 2

Coming Soon

A KING PRODUCTION

Rich
or
Famous

Rich Because You Can Buy Fame

A NOVEL

JOY DEJA KING

Welcome To My World

Before I die, if you don't remember anything else I ever taught you, know this. A man will be judged, not on what he has but how much of it. So you find a way to make money and when you think you've made enough, make some more, because you'll need it to survive in this cruel world. Money will be the only thing to save you. As I sat across from Darnell those words my father said to me on his deathbed played in my head.

"Yo, Lorenzo, are you listening to me, did you hear anything I said?"

"I heard everything you said. The problem for you is I don't give a fuck." I responded, giving a casual shoulder shrug as I rested my thumb under my chin with my index finger above my mouth.

"What you mean, you don't give a fuck? We been doing business for over three years now and that's the best you got for me?"

"Here's the thing, Darnell, I got informants all over these streets. As a matter of fact that broad you've had in your back pocket for the last few weeks is one of them."

"I don't understand what you saying," Darnell said swallowing hard. He tried to keep the tone of his voice calm, but his body composure was speaking something different.

"Alexus, has earned every dollar I've paid her to fuck wit' yo' blood suckin' ass. You a fake fuck wit' no fangs. You wanna play wit' my 100 g's like you at the casino. That's a real dummy move, Darnell." I could see the sweat beads gathering, resting in the creases of Darnell's forehead.

"Lorenzo, man, I don't know what that bitch told you but none of it is true! I swear 'bout four niggas ran up in my crib last night and took all my shit. Now that I think about it, that trifling ho Alexus probably had me set up! She fucked us both over!"

I shook my head for a few seconds not believing this muthafucker was saying that shit with a straight face. "I thought you said it was two niggas that ran up in your crib now that shit done doubled. Next thing you gon' spit is that all of Marcy projects was in on the stickup."

"Man, I can get your money. I can have it to

you first thing tomorrow. I swear!"

"The thing is I need my money right now." I casually stood up from my seat and walked towards Darnell who now looked like he had been dipped in water. Watching him fall apart in front of my eyes made up for the fact that I would never get back a dime of the money he owed me.

"Zo, you so paid, this shit ain't gon' even faze you. All I'm asking for is less than twenty-four hours. You can at least give me that," Darnell pleaded.

"See, that's your first mistake, counting my pockets. My money is *my* money, so yes this shit do faze me."

"I didn't mean it like that. I wasn't tryna disrespect you. By this time tomorrow you will have your money and we can put this shit behind us." Darnell's eyes darted around in every direction instead of looking directly at me. A good liar, he was not.

"Since you were robbed of the money you owe me and the rest of my drugs, how you gon' get me my dough? I mean the way you tell it, they didn't leave you wit' nothin' but yo' dirty draws."

"I'll work it out. Don't even stress yourself, I got you, man."

"What you saying is that the nigga you so called aligned yourself with, by using my money and my product, is going to hand it back over to you?"

"Zo, what you talking 'bout? I ain't aligned

myself wit' nobody. That slaw ass bitch Alexus feeding you lies."

"No, that's you feeding me lies. Why don't you admit you no longer wanted to work for me? You felt you was big shit and could be your own boss. So you used my money and product to buy your way in with this other nigga to step in my territory. But you ain't no boss you a poser. And your need to perpetrate a fraud is going to cost you your life."

"Lorenzo, don't do this man! This is all a big misunderstanding. I swear on my daughter I will have your money tomorrow. Fuck, if you let me leave right now I'll have that shit to you tonight!" I listened to Darnell stutter his words.

My men, who had been patiently waiting in each corner of the warehouse, dressed in all black, loaded with nothing but artillery, stepped out of the darkness ready to obliterate the enemy I had once considered my best worker. Darnell's eyes widened as he witnessed the men who had saved and protected him on numerous occasions, as he dealt with the vultures he encountered in the street life, now ready to end his.

"Don't do this, Zo! Pleeease," Darnell was now on his knees begging.

"Damn, nigga, you already a thief and a backstabber. Don't add, going out crying like a bitch to that too. Man the fuck up. At least take this bullet like a soldier."

"I'm sorry, Zo. Please don't do this. I gotta daughter that need me. Pleeease man, I'll do anything. Just don't kill me." The tears were pouring down Darnell's face and instead of softening me up it just made me even more pissed at his punk ass.

"Save your fuckin' tears. You shoulda thought about your daughter before you stole from me. You're the worse sort of thief. I invite you into my home, I make you a part of my family and you steal from me, you plot against me. Your daughter doesn't need you. You have nothing to teach her."

My men each pulled out their gat ready to attack and I put my hand up motioning them to stop. For the first time since Darnell arrived, a calm gaze spread across his face.

"I knew you didn't have the heart to let them kill me, Zo. We've been through so much together. I mean you Tania's God Father. We bigger than this and we will get through it," Darnell said, halfway smiling as he began getting off his knees and standing up.

"You're right, I don't have the heart to let them kill you, I'ma do that shit myself." Darnell didn't even have a chance to let what I said resonate with him because I just sprayed that muthafucker like the piece of shit he was. "Clean this shit up," I said, stepping over Darnell's bullet ridden body as I made my exit.

A KING PRODUCTION

Dior Comes Home...

Rich
or
Famous
Part 2

JOY DEJA KING
AND CHRIS BOOKER

Prologue

Lorenzo stepped out of his black Bugatti Coupe and entered the non-descript building in East Harlem. Normally, Lorenzo would have at least one henchman with him, but he wanted complete anonymity. When he made his entrance, the man Lorenzo planned on hiring was patiently waiting.

"I hope you came prepared for what I need."

"I wouldn't have wasted my time if I hadn't," Lorenzo stated before pulling out two pictures from a manila envelope and tossing them on the table.

"This is her?"

"Yes, her name is Alexus. Study this face very carefully, 'cause this is the woman you're going to bring to me, so I can kill."

"Are you sure you don't want me to handle it? Murder is included in my fee."

"I know, but personally killing this backstabbing snake is a gift to myself"

"Who is the other woman?"

"Her name is Lala."

"Do you want her dead, too?"

"I haven't decided. For now, just find her whereabouts and any other pertinent information. She also has a young daughter. I want you to find out how the little girl is doing. That will determine whether Lala lives or dies."

"Is there anybody else on your hit list?"

"This is it for now, but that might change at any moment. Now, get on your job, because I want results ASAP," Lorenzo demanded before tossing stacks of money next to the photos.

"I don't think there's a need to count. I'm sure it's all there," the hit man said, picking up one of the stacks and flipping through the bills.

"No doubt, and you can make even more, depending on how quickly I see results."

"I appreciate the extra incentive."

"It's not for you, it's for me. Everyone that is responsible for me losing the love of my life will pay in blood. The sooner the better."

.   Lorenzo didn't say another word and instead made his exit. He came and delivered; the rest was up to the hit man he had hired. But Lorenzo wasn't worried, he was just one of the many killers on his payroll hired to do the exact same job. He wanted to guarantee that Alexus was delivered to him alive. In his heart, he not only blamed Alexus and Lala for getting him locked up, but also held both of them responsible for Dior taking her own life. As he sat in his jail cell, Lorenzo promised himself that once he got out, if need be he would spend the rest of his life making sure both women received the ultimate retribution.

A KING PRODUCTION

DRAKE

A NOVEL

JOY DEJA KING
AND CHRIS BOOKER

Prologue

"Push! Push!" the doctor directed Kim, as he held the top of the baby's head, hoping this would be the final push that would bring a new life into the world.

The hospital's delivery room was packed with both Kim and Drake's family, and although the large crowd irritated Drake, he still managed to video record the birth of his son. After four hours of labor, Kim gave birth to a 6.5-pound baby boy, who they already named Derrick Jamal Henson Jr. Drake couldn't help but to shed a few tears of joy, at the new addition to his family, but the harsh reality of his son's safety quickly replaced his joy with anger.

Drake was nobody's angel and beyond his light brown eyes and charming smile, he was one of the most feared men in the City of Philadelphia, due to his street cred. He put a lot of work in on the blocks of South Philly, where he grew up. He mainly pushed drugs and gambled, but from time to time he'd place well-known dealers into the trunk of his car and hold them for ransom, according to how much that person was worth.

"I need everybody to leave the room for awhile." Drake told the people in the hospital room, wanting to share a private moment alone with Kim and his son.

The families took a few minutes saying their

goodbyes, before leaving. Kim and Drake sat alone in the room, rejoicing over the birth of baby Derrick. The only interruption was doctors coming in and out of the room, to check up on the baby, mainly because they were a little concerned about his breathing. The doctor informed Drake that he would run a few more tests, to make sure the baby would be fine.

"So, what are you going to do?" Kim questioned Drake, while he was cradling the baby.

"Do about what?" he shot back, without lifting his head up. Drake knew what Kim was alluding to, but he had no interest in discussing it. Once Kim became pregnant, Drake agreed to leave the street life alone, if not completely then significantly cutting back, after their baby was born. They both feared if he didn't stop living that street life, he would land in the box. Drake felt he and jail were like night and day: they could never be together.

"You know what I'm talking about, Drake. Don't play stupid with me," Kim said, poking him in his head with her forefinger.

He smiled. "I gave you my word I was out of the game when you had our baby. Unless my eyes are deceiving me, I think what I'm holding in my arms is our son. Just give me a couple days to clean up the streets and then we can sit down and come up with a plan on how to invest the money we got."

Cleaning up the streets meant selling all the drugs he had and collecting the paper owed to him from his workers and guys he fronted weight to. All together there was about 100-k due, not to mention the fact he had to appoint someone to take over his bread winning crack houses and street corners that made him millions of dollars.

Drake's thoughts came to a halt when his phone started to ring. Sending the call straight to voicemail didn't help any, because it rang again. Right when he reached to turn the phone off, he noticed it was Peaches calling. If it were anybody else, he probably would've declined, but Peaches wasn't just anybody.

"Yo," he answered, shifting the baby to his other arm, while trying to avoid Kim's eyes cutting over at him.

"He knows! He knows everything!" Peaches yelled, with terror in her voice.

Peaches wasn't getting good reception out in the woods, where Villain had left her for dead, so the words Drake was hearing were broken up. All he understood was, "Villain knows!" That was enough to get his heart racing. His heart wasn't racing out of fear, but rather excitement.

In many ways, Villain and Drake were cut from the same cloth. They even both shared tattoos of several teardrops under their eyes. It seemed like gunplay was the only thing that turned Drake on—besides fucking—and when he could feel it in the air, murder was the only thing on his mind.

Drake hung up the phone and tried to call Peaches back, to see if he could get better reception, but her phone went straight to voicemail. Damn! He thought to himself as he tried to call her back repeatedly and block out Kim's voice as she steadily asked him if everything was alright.

"Drake, what's wrong?"

"Nothing. I gotta go. I'll be back in a couple of hours,"

he said, handing Kim their son.

"How sweet! There's nothing like family!" said a voice coming from the direction of the door.

Not yet lifting his head up from his son to see who had entered the room, at first Drake thought it was a doctor, but once the sound of the familiar voice kicked in, Drake's heart began beating at an even more rapid pace. He turned to see Villain standing in the doorway, chewing on a straw and clutching what appeared to be a gun at his waist. Drake's first instinct was to reach for his own weapon, but remembering that he left it in the car made his insides burn. Surely, if he had his gun on him, there would have been a showdown right there in the hospital.

"Can I come in?" Villain asked, in an arrogant tone, as he made his way over to the visitors' chairs. "Let me start off by saying congratulations on having a bastard child."

Villain's remarks made Drake's jaw flutter continuously from fury. Sensing shit was about to go left, Kim attempted to get out of the bed with her baby to leave the room, but before her feet could hit the floor, Villain pulled out a .50 Caliber Desert Eagle and placed it on his lap. The gun was so enormous that Drake could damn near read off the serial number on the slide. Kim looked at the nurse's button and was tempted to press it.

"Push the button and I'll kill all three of y'all. Scream, and I'ma kill all three of y'all. Bitch," Villian paused, making sure the words sunk in. "if you even blink the wrong way, I'ma kill all three of y'all."

"What the fuck you want?" Drake asked, still trying to be firm in his speech.

"You know, at first, I thought about getting my money back and then killin' you, for setting my brother up wit' those bitches you got working for you. But on my way here I just said, 'Fuck the money!' I just wanna kill the nigga."

Deep down inside, Drake wanted to ask for his life to be spared, but his pride wouldn't allow it. Not even the fact that his newborn son was in the room could make Drake beg to stay alive, which made Villain more eager to lullaby his ass into a permanent sleep.

Villain wanted to see the fear in his eyes before he pulled the trigger, but Drake was a G, and was bound to play that role 'til he kissed death.

Order Form

A King Production
P.O. Box 912
Collierville, TN 38027
www.joydejaking.com
www.twitter.com/joydejaking

Name: _____

Address: _____

City/State: _____

Zip: _____

QUANTITY	TITLES	PRICE	TOTAL
_____	Bitch	$15.00	_____
_____	Bitch Reloaded	$15.00	_____
_____	The Bitch Is Back	$15.00	_____
_____	Queen Bitch	$15.00	_____
_____	Last Bitch Standing	$15.00	_____
_____	Superstar	$15.00	_____
_____	Ride Wit' Me	$12.00	_____
_____	Stackin' Paper	$15.00	_____
_____	Trife Life To Lavish	$15.00	_____
_____	Trife Life To Lavish II	$15.00	_____
_____	Stackin' Paper II	$15.00	_____
_____	Rich or Famous	$15.00	_____
_____	Rich or Famous Part 2	$15.00	_____
_____	Bitch A New Beginning	$15.00	_____
_____	Mafia Princess Part 1	$15.00	_____
_____	Mafia Princess Part 2	$15.00	_____
_____	Mafia Princess Part 3	$15.00	_____
_____	Mafia Princess Part 4	$15.00	_____
_____	Boss Bitch	$15.00	_____
_____	Baller Bitches Vol. 1	$15.00	_____
_____	Baller Bitches Vol. 2	$15.00	_____
_____	Bad Bitch	$15.00	_____
_____	Still The Baddest Bitch	$15.00	_____
_____	Power	$15.00	_____
_____	Power 2	$15.00	_____
_____	Princess Fever "Birthday Bash"	$9.99	_____

Shipping/Handling (Via Priority Mail) $6.50 1-2 Books, $8.95 3-4 Books add $1.95 for ea. Additional book.

Total: $_____ FORMS OF ACCEPTED PAYMENTS: Certified or government issued checks and money Orders, all mail in orders take 5-7 Business days to be delivered